I0626740

WITCH'N 2:
WITCHIER

WITCH'N 2:
WITCHIER

JOSHUA BRAUN

Copyright © 2025, Joshua Braun
All Rights Reserved

TABLE OF CONTENTS

Prologue	vii
Chapter 1	1
Chapter 2	13
Chapter 3	19
Chapter 4	29
Chapter 5	37
Chapter 6	45
Chapter 7	55
Chapter 8	63
Chapter 9	71
Chapter 10	77
Chapter 11	85
Chapter 12	93
Chapter 13	103
Chapter 14	113
Chapter 15	119
Chapter 16	125
Chapter 17	131
Chapter 18	143
Chapter 19	149
Chapter 20	157

Chapter 21   163
Chapter 22   173
Chapter 23   179
Chapter 24   187
Chapter 25   195
Chapter 26   205
Epilogue   213
About The Author   215

PROLOGUE

There are many universes of many different kinds. Most are similar. The same laws of physics, the same rules that resulted in stars and planets and the occasional inconvenient occurrence of life. Others on the other hand are difficult to understand without a specific cocktail of drugs and even then, understanding is often fleeting.

Universes can come in all sizes, from so small that we could not perceive them with our most powerful devices to being a great deal larger than a duck. That said, we're in one of the biggest ones. Not big enough to draw many tourists. Just shy of the top one hundred list. People like to go and visit every universe on the list, but the only ones who come to old one hundred and one just do it for a laugh. It doesn't help that our universe is mostly empty space. It's not unusual; lots of places are like that, but the ninety-eighth biggest universe has rivers of whipped cream connecting planets. The rivers are also populated by cream merpeople who love performing oral sex. It's hard to compete with that.

Among the endless universes in the cosmos existed one universe that held three planets that did not move at all. Around these planets rotated two creatures that most would call gods.

One of goodness, and one of evil. They fought their constant battle against each other, a stalemate that lasted hundreds of thousands of years. Until the god of goodness concocted a plan to win the war. She withdrew into herself for many decades. Evil nearly conquered all three planets and people believed the goddess had abandoned them.

When at last she emerged she did so with a new angel she'd formed. One so perfect and so well wrought that she eclipsed the power of both gods. The evil god could never consider such a plan, for if he made a creature more powerful than himself it would surely betray him.

The angel fought back the forces of darkness, tireless and unstoppable. She threw down the evil god from the sky and smote him in the darkness below. The universe with its three planets became a paradise where only goodness reigned.

The angel sat in the center of them, unmoving, unchanging. So she thought it would be for all eternity.

The universe remained, happily ever after—nearly. For one day, a witch drunkenly crashed into the universe, and for a brief time chaos came to the paradise once again. The long-standing harmony unbalanced.

Once the witch left, fully satisfied with the fun she'd had, the universe would stabilize, but the angel would never be the same.

CHAPTER 1

Honeydrops, the witch, former ruler of the world, most powerful creature in the entire cosmos, currently sat on the courthouse steps alone in the late evening. The sun cast a warm glow over the town and over the courthouse, which sat just on its northernmost edge. The newest addition to the town, which did not often get new additions.

This day it held the distinct honor of being the agreed-upon meeting place for the representatives of two different kingdoms. Trouble had stewed between the two of them, and so Honeydrops was summoned to come and attend negotiations so the matter could be put to bed.

The witch, for her part, hated her life. Her beauty, still mostly unearthly, but now less so. Even eternally young, the most beautiful can still be worn down by time and stress. While yes, somewhere underneath it all she still held an ethereal appeal, nineteen years of misery and struggle had done their damage.

Bags have formed under her eyes. While she has been meaning for some time to schedule a spa day, time is a ruthless bitch. Since accepting stewardship over the world she once, mostly, destroyed, she'd been left little time for leisure and her once flawless skin often broke out into rashes and at the worst of it, even hives. Her hair, always a bit wild, lost much of its luster and color. The white at her roots, more grayish, and the black at her tips less shiny. The orange and green in between dull instead of toxic. The volume just plain gone as it lay flat against her head.

Keeping peace and justice across the entire world did not keep anyone in good health or in good spirits. For you see, even without an evil witch terrorizing the world, people were, to put it bluntly, often selfish, stupid, petty assholes.

Worst of all, her daughter, whom she loved more than anything in the world, left her on the quest to find her father. Honey had always meant to tell Mathew about their daughter, but between trying to hold the world together and being a single mom, she'd never found the right time. If she were being honest with herself, which she wasn't, she might admit she'd feared her daughter might opt for the more stable life her father could provide.

Inevitability came, despite all attempts to prevent it. She'd hugged her daughter close one last time, made her promise to never kill her mother, and said goodbye. Watching until the girl disappeared from view, even as it put her behind schedule.

The day's negotiations were, as politics were more often than not, painfully boring. She suffered through because, well, she owed it to everyone. Having killed roughly three-fourths of the population of the planet either directly or through her actions incurred a moral debt that could never truly be repaid. So she sat through the boredom, idly scratching the rash on her neck. Ignoring, or rather, trying to ignore the rash that formed in a thin line just below her left boob.

Ignoring it made it worse, which made her sweat, which made it even worse. Eventually she grabbed a book and tried to rub it inconspicuously below her boob while pretending to read it. It's the sort of desperate plan that forms in one's mind when they're too distracted by discomfort to realize it's never going to work. She hoped no one noticed. They did, but no one said anything.

Occasionally some tyrant might rise through a coup or just by having enough idiots to support them that no one tried to stop them until too late. These occasions broke up the boredom and allowed her to let off some steam. They were rare, however, and she'd taken to not killing loads of people anymore so she couldn't let off too much steam. "Nothing like a bit of mass murder to start the day off," one of her old demon friends used to say after they'd engaged in just such an activity.

You might think, how could anyone be stupid enough to try a power grab with an all-powerful witch keeping things in check? Well, I refer you back to the stupid, selfish, petty asshole comment. On top of that, the sort of person who thinks to themselves, "Yeah, I should be in charge of everything," is the sort of narcissist who looks at untamable power and says, "I think I got this."

Honeydrops had once been this exact sort of person, except she could back it up with facts. She'd traveled across universes, and dimensions, and to places that were neither. After centuries of having fun, or, more accurately, engaging in reckless self-destruction to avoid the task her mother enforced on her, she finally did what she'd been born to do. Only, it hadn't worked out, and now she'd been serving her penance for nearly nineteen years. Which, given the scale and scope of her reign of terror, didn't amount to diddly-squat.

She'd made one critical error, however, in thinking that after her travels she could just come home and no one would ever come looking for her. Which brings us to the moment when Honey sat alone on the courthouse steps, regretting, not for the first time, ever listening to her mother. A brief moment of peace at the end of the day before she had to move on to the next task, the next summon, the next crisis. In such moments she often felt sorry for herself, then felt guilty for feeling sorry since she didn't think she deserved any pity. Wishing she'd made so many different choices, and lamenting that even with all her power, she could not undo what is done.

Lost in her misery she didn't notice the distant figure that walked along the now deserted road of the town toward her. A robe of darkness covered the entirety of the figure, the hood hanging low to obscure the face. And when I say darkness, I mean real dark, like have you seen Vantablack? That's the kind of darkness I mean. If you don't know

Vantablack, look it up on the Internet. If you don't have the Internet, then that probably means my generation couldn't do enough to save the world and society collapsed. I'm sorry, but I am a little thankful my book survived the apocalypse.

Suffice it to say, when a figure in a robe of darkness walks along a road, it clears up pretty quick. This is doubly true if you're living in a fantasy universe where figures in black robes are almost always up to no good. The best you can hope for is some kind of antihero and trouble always seems to find those sorts.

As a result, when the figure stood fifteen feet away, Honey finally looked up to see the figure walking toward her on the recently deserted road. They regarded each other, the figure almost seven and a half feet tall. Honey, diminutive compared to most people, sitting on the steps looked very small indeed. The figure drew back its hood, revealing a face of dark gold. Beautiful like a leopard, yet stern and unyielding. Her eyes solid gold orbs of light, metallic in their appearance, but a changing metal as if melted and run down only to solidify before melting again, the light inside pulsing faintly like a heartbeat. Around her head were tight curls of light that created a bright halo that made the shadows of her face look deeper.

"Melissa?" Honey said, surprised by the person she'd departed from nearly a century ago, both making it very clear they never wanted to see the other ever again.

Melissa, as it may not surprise you, was not her name. Melicintarifer, the angel whose power eclipsed her god, threw back her robe, revealing her feathered wings of golden red burning in brilliant light that would cause most to turn away from their holy glare. The wings arched upward, ten feet tall and dragged on the ground where they left a burning trail. They unfurled in a massive wingspan blazing brighter and larger than the sun. A metal plate of white gold, etched in fire, covered every inch of her. The armor did not exist to protect her, but to contain her divine radiance, so powerful that if it were not contained it would set the area around her on fire.

She pulled her sword from the air, it's blade nearly as long as the angel who wielded it. She held it up in front of her, blocking half her face. The center of the blade a fire blazing bright and its edges molten flame that flowed around it like a river. The angel pointed the blade at Honey.

"Oh, shit," Honey said with the sort of casual concern of someone who dropped something but wasn't going to bother picking it up. The sky shook, and reality rent. From the fissures poured white and gold flames. And well, long story short, that was the end of that town hall. A pity given it had been built only five years ago. Which, ya know, isn't new new, but it still had many good years ahead of it.

A lot of golden waves of flame that covered the sun clashed with purple lightning that rent the planet to its core. Along with a good deal of screaming, shouting, and powers that made gods in their heavens tremble. At the end of it the two ended up as they always did: naked, cuddling, and covered in the ash of the wasted landscape around them.

Melicintarifer muttered to herself, not for the first time, "Damn it, I did it again."

So, let's go back a bit, several centuries ago, to when these two first met. It started after the witch got drunk—this being the event that made her swear off alcohol—and then got kicked of the fae dimensions. The reason why, well, as she would put it when failing to defend herself later, "You playfully suggest eating one person and suddenly no one wants you around anymore. What's up with that?"

In a fit of self-pity and total disregard for any rules of magic, or any rules of reality, she bounced around in the place between. A place that doesn't actually exist and yet must exist, because something must separate all that useless shit we call existence. When the rules finally managed to catch up with the witch, they ejected her into the nearest place they could.

There's really no telling exactly how much damage she caused to the place between, but if your reality happened to be invaded by some sort of unspeakable horror around this time or if the laws of physics went all wonky for a few seconds there's a good chance she's to blame.

When she finally landed, she found herself in paradise, which isn't bad considering what she'd just been up to. In this place of pure goodness, no one wanted to approach this stranger who didn't look to be in all that great a state and kept slurring her words while mumbling about cannibalism really not being THAT big of a deal. So the task fell to the most powerful creature in the realm, Melicintarifer.

The angel approached the witch—tall, beautiful, and terrible, standing above short, disheveled, and not able to stand up without wavering around. "Stranger, why have you come to this place?" the angel asked, her very voice causing nature to shiver from her power.

The witch, not fully clear on her situation, took a long and overly lecherous look at the angel and said, "Hey, good-looking, wanna have some fun? Some sexy, sexy fun, just to be clear. Flirting with women as a woman can be hard to get through to. I just want to be clear."

No one had ever asked the angel this question because most people had the sense not to. Nor did anyone ever look at the angel in this fashion, partly out of respect for her divinity and partly because parts of her were brighter than the sun.

This did result in a new curiosity arising in the angel. She did understand such things, but never thought before she might engage in them. Melicintarifer simply hadn't been formed for such activities. Yet her power eclipsed her creator and with this new curiosity her body started to change. Not fully, not yet, but it began something. She opened her mouth to say, "No," but being a good angel she couldn't lie. The answer wasn't no, but it wasn't yes, so she said, "Not now."

The witch winked, and said, "Alright, let me know when you're ready," then slapped the angel on the ass, which gave a clank since it was covered in armor. The angel, not understanding the witch's intent, took this as an attack, and drew her sword. The two fought, but the witch, being drunk, stupid, and horny, took the angel's fighting as flirting, and thus, began flirting back.

Honey hadn't quite yet achieved her full power at this time, but could still match the angel one for one. All her life Melicintarifer had only encountered things weaker than her. Meeting someone just as strong made for yet another curiosity. Their fight lasted days, throughout which Honey never stopped flirting, despite sobering up and going through a truly heinous hangover. Melicintarifer did prove victorious in the end, since being an angel she did not need rest or food, and while Honey's magic gave her the power to forgo a lot. Spending most of the power flirt fighting did cause her to give out eventually. Even lying on the ground, exhausted, Honey kept hitting on the angel. The angel drew close to the witch, who reached up and caressed her cheek, thinking they were about to kiss. No one, save her god, had ever touched Melicintarifer. Not even the other angels could withstand her power.

The shock of it caused the angel to drop her defenses, which allowed Honey to pull her in for a kiss. The two ended up as they are now, naked, cuddling, and covered in ash from the devastated landscape around them. Melicintarifer filled with regret at what she'd just done.

Thus began a long and very toxic story of enemies to lovers, to enemies, to lovers, to enemies, to lovers, and well, you get the idea.

Back in the present, Honey gave a long sigh, and traced a finger down the center of the angel's body. "I really needed that."

"I didn't come here for this." Melissa stood up, and with a burst of holy radiance, cleared herself of the ash and fluids covering her body. Her holy armor flew back to her and covered her up.

"Yeah, yeah. You always say that, but every time you show up it's only a matter of time before you're begging to take a prolonged trip to my vagina." Honey made an inappropriate gesture at the appropriate area. Standing up as well, she reached into the ashen earth and pulled a torrent of it up from the ground. Wrapping the torrent around her body, it turned into a black halter dress. "It would be nice if you didn't burn my clothes off for once. I'd love to stick around for another round—"

"There won't be another round; this is the last time this ever happens." Melissa's eyes blazed brighter as Honey rolled hers. "I came here to … to put an end to your dark existence. The terror and destruction you've caused across several universes, including my own." Melissa drew her sword again.

"Baby, you need to stop lying to yourself, and put that thing away. I said I don't have time for another round. I have to get some sleep for the peace conference tomorrow." Honey swirled her hands around, and the devastated landscape regrew around them, trees and green grass returning.

"Spare me your lies; you don't do peace conferences … or sleep."

"A lot's changed since we last saw each other. Thanks though; I missed you." Honey gave Melissa a swat on her armored ass and started to walk away.

"That's it?" Melissa's wings hummed in the air, sounding almost like music as she floated behind Honey. "You tell me you have a peace conference and you're just leaving?"

"I'm super busy these days and honestly I just can't with you right now."

"You can't with me? YOU CAN'T WITH ME?!" Melissa's golden eyes flared and the curls of light on her head turned to flames.

"Yeah, that's what I said." Honey shrugged. "Ironic, huh?"

"You are unbelievable."

"Unbelievably sexy maybe," Honey said, but her heart wasn't in it.

"Why do I do this to myself? Why do I keep doing this to myself?" Melissa said, taking to the sky. "I'm leaving."

"Hey, maybe give me a little warning next time; I'm super busy these days."

Melissa whirled around in the air and came back. "I am not coming back, do you hear me? This is never happening again."

Honey rolled her eyes yet again. "Oh, please, you got a taste of Honey once and you've never been able to stay away since."

"As usual, nothing you say makes any sense."

"Honey, my name, it's a pun."

Melissa's feet touched the ground. "Your name is Honey."

"Honeydrops is my full name, but yeah."

"You always refused to tell me your name; why now?"

"Holy shit that's right, I never told you. Well everyone knows it now." Honey walked past Melissa once again, who shook her head.

"Unbelievable. All that time, I begged you to tell me and now you TELL EVERYONE!"

"It's a long story, but the short of it is I came back home to fulfill my dream, or rather my mom's dream of conquering the world. I got bored, so I gave up evil and have reformed my ways."

"You, gave up evil, because you were bored?" Melissa grabbed at the light around her head. "So, all those times, I begged you to come with me. To stop all the things you were doing, and you did it, because you were bored?"

"There's more to it than that, but basically, yeah."

"I don't know why I bother with you."

"I don't know why either. Oh yeah, my irresistible vagina."

Melissa followed behind Honey, her wings leaving a burnt trail behind her. "It's because I love you, damn it, but that just isn't enough for you."

"You don't love me, and you never have. You just gave into your lust for the first Goth hottie you met and because you couldn't handle it you needed to rationalize it as love. Don't feel bad; you're not the first."

"No, Honeydrops." Melissa smiled at saying her name. "I do love you, but you just can't believe someone like me could love someone like you. This time, I am well and truly done with you."

"I have a daughter."

"The fuck?"

Honey stopped and turned to look at the angel. "Whoa, I've never heard you swear before."

"How? I thought that couldn't happen unless you wanted it to."

"Subconsciously, I think I did. I fell in love."

"You did? Who is he?"

"Oh no, not him; he sucks. But with his mom."

Melissa pinched the top of her nose. "OK, I don't know what weird incestuous thing you got into this time, but I want nothing to do with it."

"It wasn't like that, and besides the incest thing was one time. Everyone wants to try it with twins."

"What twins? Who are you talking about?"

"Who are *you* talking about?" Honey asked.

"Joseph, Josephine, and Joseph Jr."

Honey stopped to remember the three people. "They were related? Oh, that's disgusting?"

"I KNOW!"

"Now that you say it, it does make sense with the names. Anyway, Alma and I were strictly platonic. She died."

"And you had sex with her son?"

"I was drunk," Honey said. "By accident," she added with emphasis.

"Can I meet her?"

"I told you she died."

"Your daughter, idiot."

Honey hugged her arm. "You really want to?"

"Yes, of course."

"She's off looking for her father and I have a busy schedule making up for destroying the world."

"What about all the other places you've destroyed?"

"Yeah, I know, there's an extensive list of my fuckups, but I can only be one place at a time."

Melissa let a gauntlet drop from her hand and stroked Honey's cheek. "You're really trying aren't you?"

Honey closed her eyes at the angel's touch, but pulled away. "I don't have room in my life for more complications."

"I'm a complication?"

"We're a complication. I … we've tried, and it doesn't work."

"OK, well, we'll go to your peace conference tomorrow and then we'll meet your daughter. Then, if you want me to, I'll go."

Honey didn't really want her to go, but she also didn't believe she would stay. "I've so much to do, so much to make up for. I can't just take a break."

"You can take a break, for me."

She almost said no, but the long boring years had worn on her. Melissa always came back, and always left. Right now, she thought if she dared to think it might be different it could break her, and she lacked the strength to survive it this time. She also didn't have the strength to say no to the one person she wanted most in the world to be by her side. "OK, fine, for you."

CHAPTER 2

With her dark hair and dark skin, Alma, Honey's daughter, sat at the table, bouncing her heels. Alteem poured a cup of tea for her, but didn't offer any sugar.

"How much did your mother tell you about me?" Alteem asked, pouring himself a cup and sitting across from her.

"That she killed your whole family and destroyed your kingdom and nearly all of its people. Then she tortured you for a long time before you went on a road trip together."

Alteem scratched the mostly gray beard at his chin. "That about sums it up."

"So, where's Mathew, my father?" Alma took a drink of the tea, but took too much and ended up dribbling some back into the cup lest the heat burn her.

"He moved away after his mother died. He teaches at a university up north in Waluigia."

"Guess, I'm off there then." Alma got up.

"Wait, you've only just got here."

Alma sat down again. "Right, sorry, we were always rushing off from one place to another. Trying to keep the world together after she destroyed everything. Not used to sticking around."

"What do you … how have you … can you do magic?"

"Oh yeah, let me show you?" Alma's eyes lit up with excitement as she pulled out a deck of cards from her pocket and fanned them out. "Pick a card, any card."

Alteem stared at the cards. "That's OK, I'm sure you're great at it."

She put the cards away, her face sinking.

"I'll be honest," Alteem continued, "I don't know how to process this."

"Sorry, didn't really wish to drop all this on you all at once, but there's no good way to tell people about this sort of thing."

"How was it being raised by ... her?"

"Mom is very loving and supportive, a bit clingy." Alma had some more of her tea, slurping it a little too loudly.

"That's good; she didn't have the best childhood herself."

Alma laughed. "I know. It's strange to say, so many people know her as this terrible thing, but it's hard to picture my mom is the person everyone says she is. There's a whole generation that's grown up now only knowing her as a protector."

Alteem had never thought of that. Once children everywhere lived in terror of the witch who scoured the world. Now, if bad things were happening Honey arrived to save them. Those who'd lived through her atrocities could never forget them, but those who hadn't ...

"I think I'll go with you," Alteem said.

"Really?" Alma perked up, surprised.

"Yeah, I'm not so old that I can't have one more adventure."

"How old are you anyway? It was really unclear in the stories Mom told me."

"About twenty-seven at the end of the war. Honey only ruled the world for a few years, but I lost track of time then. I'd guess thirty or thirty-one by the time I met your grandmother. She was probably four years older than me. Though our troubles made us both look older than we were."

"I did not know that."

"Yeah, about ten years passed before Honey showed up in my life again. It's been eighteen years since then, so I'm roughly fifty-eight or fifty-nine."

"OK, that makes sense," Alma said. (And I hope everyone's happy now I've cleared that up.) "When will you be ready to go?"

"I'll need a bit of time to put my affairs in order, but I can be ready in a week."

"That long?"

"Yes, is that a problem?"

"It's fine, I'm just used to always being on the road. I'm sure there's something I can do around town. As Mom always said, there's always someone who needs help and we can be the someone who helps them."

"Your mom said that?"

"Of course, she's always saying stuff like that."

"Of course, that sounds just like her." Alteem thought back on a few of his less pleasant memories of the witch. "You can stay here of course, until we're ready to leave. I'll set up the spare bedroom for you."

"Righty tighty," Alma said, getting up. "I'm off to do some good deeds."

Alma went to the town and moved through it, doing good deeds with such speed and efficiency that it could it only be described as a hurricane of benevolence, which is sort of the opposite of a regular hurricane.

She found people in need and helped them with such immediate ease that to witness it one must think something preternatural occurred. This indeed was the case, for as much as Honeydrops, even from a young age, showed an inhuman talent for chaos and destruction, so did her daughter have a talent for harmony and restoration. The magic she worked in daily routine so subtle that not even she or her mother noticed. Guided by magic through her unconscious will to be at the right place at the right time always. Even moving through space without noticing it, being in different areas far faster than she should be. You think she might notice, but she'd always been like that.

15

No one had really completely noticed the full effect of her presence since, traveling with her mother, she scarcely stayed anywhere more than a day. After a week, though, the old village looked and behaved like the sort of impossibly idyllic place that only exists in bad fantasy novels just before something terrible happens. You know the sort that usually results in an orphan or two having to swear revenge. Nothing like that happened here, and Alteem alone noticed the change since he observed mostly from the outside.

She did wander into his classroom at one point, followed by one of the children's lost puppies that she'd just so happened to find, and carrying a basket of cookies that a baker had given her in thanks for helping out when their child had a cold. Alma, naturally, shared them with the class since she'd never be able to eat them all. Briefly, she helped a student with a problem he'd never been quite able to get, and left in a breeze of sweet smells and warm wind.

Alteem also observed that it never rained while she stayed there, but everywhere it looked like spring after a fresh rain for the duration of her stay. The sun always shone, and it stayed warm, never hot, with a gentle breeze and the smell of flowers always in her passing.

He did try to hint to Alma a couple of times to see what she might say, but the girl always dismissed such things with a bright smile and a cheesy quote from her mother about helping people. "Helping others makes the sun shine in our hearts," she'd say, when he pointed out that the sun always shone around her but never managed to get in her eyes. Rooms even got brighter whenever she entered them.

All in all, much like her mother, the laws of reality changed around Alma, but in entirely different ways.

The end of the week came, Alteem having settled his affairs. Alma woke up with perfect hair, fantastic breath, and smelling sweet.

"You don't carry anything with you when you travel?" Alteem noted.

"I always manage to find what I need whenever I need it." Alma shrugged.

"Right, of course." Alteem started on the road with Alma following behind and humming a lighthearted tune.

The day started out quite expectedly perfect. The sun was shining, but clouds granted them a comfortable shade. Alteem did not remember the road being so lined with flowers before.

Some hours onto the road a carriage passed them. Several trunks covered the back and two passengers rode in front of it. A man in a suit with a top hat drove the horses and a younger woman, likely a daughter, wore a bonnet beside him.

Alma gave them a wave and a smile as they passed. The carriage made its way ahead of them, close to disappearing from view. Out in the distance a group of four bandits appeared, riding out of the woods. They closed in on the carriage, which did not notice them until too late. They snatched several of the trunks and began to ride off.

"I wish we could do something, but there's no way we'll catch them," Alma said. "If only we had a horse of our own."

Just then, seemingly from nowhere, a unicorn rode up next to Alma. Its back half was that of a deer with its front half being a horse. It had a white coat and a rainbow shimmer in its hair. Its horn one of a twirling white shine.

"Oh, dear unicorn, some bandits have taken off with the luggage of those unfortunate people up ahead on the road." Alma gestured ahead of them on the road. "Would you be willing to let me ride you so I can attempt to retrieve it?"

The unicorn tossed its head in affirmation, then bent down so Alma could hoist herself onto its back. They rode off, her hair trailing behind her in the wind as she rode. A path of flowers followed in the unicorns wake. The sun illuminating them with a glow as they galloped together.

Alteem briefly wondered what the girl intended as he began a steady jog along the road to eventually catch up. She could not stop all the bandits on her own, but he saw her call out to them. They halted at her voice and she rode up alongside them, the sun and the wind catching in her hair.

Starting to sweat, Alteem continued his jog as he watched Alma converse with the bandits. They looked enraptured by her, and Alteem had to admit anyone would be. It's not every day a beautiful girl appears riding on a unicorn. The sun going out of its way to illuminate her with a glow.

He'd managed to cover maybe half the distance when the bandits took the trunks back to the carriage. As they arrived at the carriage more words were exchanged. The carriage driver started to ask some questions and as the lead bandit answered the driver burst into tears. Alma took each of them by the hand and spoke to them further. The driver embraced the bandit and he joined them in the carriage as his fellows followed behind. The party continued on its way as Alma returned on the unicorn. She got down off it, hugged it and offered thanks before the unicorn leaped into the air and disappeared.

"So, everything worked out then?" Alteem asked catching his breath.

"Yes, I caught up to the bandits and explained to them they shouldn't be stealing. They said they had no other way to survive, so I promised to help them if they returned the luggage. They agreed and we returned to the carriage. One of the bandits had a locket around his neck, and it turned out he's the long-lost nephew of the carriage driver. You see, he lost track of his pregnant sister during Mom's dark reign. He eventually gave her and her baby up for dead, and while she did die the baby survived. The only thing he had of his mother was her amulet that he kept all these years, which is how the carriage driver recognized him. It turns out, the carriage driver is on his way to a town because his daughter is marrying a man in the construction business. As it just so happens, he needs four more men to help him out so they'll all be able to get jobs with him. Good thing that unicorn showed up or none of them would have ever known."

"Yup, sure was," Alteem said. A different person likely would react more to such a story or even Alteem at a different point in his life. Except he had lived through the destruction of the world, and its restoration. He'd watched the worst person in the world slowly reform. Now, somehow, that same worst person had managed to raise an elemental force of goodness. Experience had taught him to roll with it. "Do you encounter unicorns often?"

"From time to time."

CHAPTER 3

Seven nations attended the peace conference, all sitting around a table. Many an eye glanced to the angel of dark gold who stood in the corner holding her wings at an awkward angle to avoid setting the building on fire. Honey did little, as the leaders discussed things. Mostly she sat bored out of her mind, which made for her default state these days. Years ago, she'd needed to do a lot. The world had been rent asunder, specifically by her, and putting it back together proved a monumental task. She'd done that, helping nations draw lines, set up governments, repair infrastructure. The rebuilding continued, but the systems were in place now. They only required her presence, which reminded everyone to behave.

The business of the day finished when trade treaties were renewed or renegotiated, along with border policies, and international laws. People shook hands and began milling about as their official duties were done.

"Is this what you do now?" Melissa asked approaching a half-asleep Honey who snapped up at the question.

She blinked the sleep out of her eyes. "It's all anyone needs of me anymore."

"I never thought you'd have the patience for it."

"I don't."

"Yet you stay." Melissa looked at the people around the room. "You've really changed."

"Yeah, it sucks." Honey got to her feet and stretched. "OK well, that's done."

Stekabrim, her current assistant, approached. "Honey," he said holding a piece of paper, "there's a request for you to help settle a dispute across the ocean." There'd been many assistants over the years. None stayed around for long since they all accepted the job for a good look on their résumés. They lasted a year or two before moving on to more stable work.

Honey deflated, sinking back down into the chair. "Alright."

"No," Melissa said. "She's taking a break from her duties to travel with me."

Stekabrim stuttered with surprise and looked to Honey. The witch shrugged as if to say the angel is the boss.

"Good, now that's settled, let's go." Melissa motioned for Honey to follow as she walked out of the room.

"Damn," said Honey catching up to the angel. "How come you're never like that in bed?"

Melissa went stiff and looked back into the room to see if anyone heard.

"What?" said Honey. "It was hot; I like to be the bottom sometimes is all I'm saying."

"Do you have to discuss our sex life in public?"

"I don't *have* to, why?"

Melicintarifer gave the witch a harsh look. "It's embarrassing."

"Oh, like we've never had sex in public?"

"Quiet! No one needs to know about that."

"I think a lot of people know about that; they were there."

The angel sighed. "Why are you always like this?"

"It's just who I am. It's why everybody, including you, hates me."

"I don't hate you. I never have."

"Well you should, because I have killed so many babies, and whatever you think the number is I promise it's way higher."

20

Melissa cupped Honey's face and stroked it with her thumb. "Awww, you finally understand that it's wrong to kill babies."

Honey brushed Melissa's hand away. "That should not be your takeaway from what I just said."

"I always believed someday you could change." A single tear of fire dripped down Melissa's cheek and singed the ground. "I'm so happy."

"Whatever. It's just a matter of time before you leave again so we might as well just get freaky as frequently as possible before the inevitable happens, because I am pent up." Melissa always leaves, Honey said to herself; Melissa always comes back. "There's a supply closet right here and be warned I will not be quiet." Honey opened the door to the supply closet and gestured inside.

Melissa bit her lip and wanted to give in, but she did not want to validate Honey's statement. So she patted Honey on the forehead, and kissed her. "If you're really trying to be better, then I'm not leaving, because I love you," she said, then walked past and headed outside.

"Wha … you get back here right now and have sex with me to prove you don't love me." Honey scratched her head. "Wow, how many times have I said that in my life?"

When Melissa did not return for the sex Honey gave in and followed her outside. A hundred blasts of light exploded around Honey as soon as she stepped out the door. In the sky a red spaceship hovered, a frame a mile long, sleek and thin in the shape of a cylinder that narrowed near its tip with six rocket engines on the back and three fins spaced evenly. A slew of plasma batteries were firing at Honey, their blasts exploding on impact.

The batteries were eventually forced to pause their attack as their barrels, glowing red, needed to cool down. Honey, of course, remained unharmed, but she stood in a crater with everything around her destroyed. "Fucking fuck," she said. "Is this just a thing that's going to keep happening now? Every time I come out of a building someone's going to be waiting to attack me?"

"Who is that?" Melissa asked, not having even the slightest cause to worry about Honey's safety.

"I don't know, you've got the wings; you fly up and ask them."

So Melissa did, returning shortly. "It's some guy who says he's hunted you across a hundred universes. He's the last survivor of a people you've killed."

"That is really not specific enough."

"You want me to tell him that?"

Honey looked up to the spaceship with the fading red of its guns. "I guess."

"I think it will upset him."

"Really? What do you think I should say?" The batteries resumed their assault before being forced to pause again. "This is no way to have a conversation. Go tell him it doesn't matter how many times he does that; it's not going to work."

"OK." Melissa once again flew up before returning. "He doesn't believe you. He thinks it has to wear you down eventually."

"It's magic, damn it; it doesn't follow logical rules." The barrage resumed again for its duration. "Is it just the one guy?"

"Yes, the rest of the ship is just robots."

"Sentient robots or are we talking automation?"

"You want me to ask?"

"Please do."

One final time Melissa took the journey. "Yeah, they're automated."

"Can you do me a favor?"

"Of course."

"Catch." Honey's eyes glowed their toxic green, her hands crackled with purple energy. Stretching them out, a beam of deep purple shot into the sky, striking the ship. Purple lightning cracked around the ship, which shuddered in the sky before vanishing, leaving only a man who fell from the sky. Melissa flew up and caught him, bringing him back down.

His head a glass bowl with two antennae sticking out of the top. A skin-tight space suit of mustard yellow covered his body showing off some taut-ass muscles all over his body including his taut ass muscles. Red gloves and boots covered his hands and feet and as soon as Melissa put him down he drew a ray gun, a torpedo-looking thing with three rings around it, and fired at Honey. It, of course, did nothing.

"Seriously?" Honey said.

"Your defenses must give way eventually. You committed genocide against my people on Pentacerous 5." He made motions with the ray gun as if doing so might make it shoot harder. "I shall avenge them or die trying. I swore to it."

"First, near genocide, because, come on, you're standing right here. Clearly I missed one."

Melissa covered her face with a gauntleted hand.

"Vile creature," the man said. "You mock my pain, but after learning how to travel across universes I shall at last have justice."

"Second," Honey continued, "I'm sorry for the near genocide, and this might upset you, but I have no idea who you are."

"You ..." The man stopped ray gunning her. "You destroyed my whole life. How can you not remember?"

"That just doesn't narrow it down a whole lot. Help me out; was my hair this color?"

"Yes."

"OK, did we have sex?"

Melissa let out a groan.

The man looked from Honey to Melissa. "Why would I have sex with someone who killed all my people?"

"Sometimes it's better when you hate the other person. Melissa here knows what I'm talking about." Honey nudged Melissa.

"You're actually the only person I've ever been with," Melissa said, avoiding looking at the man.

"Right and you hate me, remember?"

Melissa shook her head.

"I've never had sex with anyone. Everyone was dead," the man said. "I did meet some people traveling across the cosmos, but never the right one."

"OK, so, if I have sex with you will that make up for the near genocide?"

"Honey, no," Melissa said.

"Who are you?" the man asked the angel.

"I'm her girlfriend."

"Oh, so after everything you've done you get a hot angel girlfriend. That's not fair." The man tried to ray gun Honey even harder.

"She pretends she's my girlfriend," Honey said.

"So," the man said, putting his hands on his hips and looking at Melissa, "is she any good at sex?"

Melissa bit her lip and shuffled her feet. "I don't think that's an appropriate question."

"No, I'd like to hear the answer," Honey said.

"Well …," Melissa said.

Honey fell to her knees and threw her arms up in the air. "Damn it, I knew it. I screw up everything."

"No, no, I like it, it's just, your nails are very sharp. Although, not this last time."

"Yeah, they fell out from stress when I had an infant daughter and a postapocalyptic world to take care of at the same time. They came back normal after a decade or so."

"Damn, OK," the man said.

"Be honest, how often do you climax?" Honey asked.

"A lot," Melissa said. "At least one out of every three times we did it."

"That's terrible." Honey fell the rest of the way to the ground. "Maybe not for a straight couple, but we're lesbians."

"I'm a lesbian," Melissa said. "You're more of an omnisexual nymphomaniac. Also you know, even positive stereotypes can be harmful. The idea that lesbians make better couples can put pressure on people if things aren't going well and make it easier to ignore abuse. I don't want to high road you or anything, but, you know, be aware."

"You'd think I'd be better at sex after having so much."

"Don't worry about it, I just like being with you."

"That is not helping. You deserve better. Just bury me in a hole and forget about me."

"I uh," the man began, holstering his ray gun. "I didn't expect you to be such a ..."

"Trash fire of a person," Honey offered.

"Yeah." The man cleared his throat. "I'm not really interested in sex, just more curious about the answer."

"Are you sure? You could still have a go, roll the dice on those one-out-of-three odds. I'm already lying here."

"No, really. I wouldn't be able to live with myself afterward. Trading sex in recompense for genocide feels a bit, shitty."

Honey got back to her feet. "If it makes you feel any better I've never been able to live with myself."

The man nodded. "Yeah it does. I came here for revenge, but seeing you like this is honestly better. You're suffering for your crimes."

"Yup," Honey said with a wink and smile as she got back to her feet. "I've fucked up my life and nothing will ever make it any better. I realize that now."

"That's not true," Melissa said, taking one of Honey's hands.

"Don't mind her." Honey pulled her hand free. "She's an angel; they're all delusional."

"Right." The man looked around. "Don't suppose you could point me to the nearest spaceport."

"We don't have those here. No one in this universe has invented space travel. They're not even at an industrial age yet. It's not the worst though; most industrial ages are true hellholes. Granted preindustrial societies can sometimes have a real human rights problem, but then I suppose so can a lot of postindustrial societies. Really there's just no winning."

"Can you take me to a universe that does have space travel?"

Honey let out an awkward sigh. "During the next winter solstice sure. I absolutely can. I could do it sooner, but not without, you know, sacrificing an infant and I don't do that anymore. Melissa, sweetie, what about you?"

"I can only transport people with a pure heart, or that are invulnerable like Honey here. Otherwise the divine power would crush you." Melissa patted Honey on the shoulder. "Can you make him invulnerable?"

"Well, yes and no. So, in order to use it on someone who isn't my bloodline I'd need to ..."

"Sacrifice a baby."

"Yeah, you guessed it."

"How much of your magic revolves around sacrificing babies?" the man asked.

"Not as much as it seems like right now. These are just some big asks. Interuniversal travel and invulnerability are some serious laws of nature-breaking stuff. There are other ways of course, but when your family's been evil for generations and there are babies lying around everywhere it doesn't incentivize seeking out those other ways."

"How long till the winter solstice?"

"Seven months."

"Doesn't that mean the summer solstice is just a month away?"

Honey clapped her hands together. "Oh, I can get you out of here on the summer solstice. Just not to somewhere with space travel, or rather, nowhere you'd want to be. Worms, fading suns, so many different fascist states, and other weird shit."

"Is there anywhere else to go that's not a dystopia?"

Honey thought about it. "Some heavens, I suppose."

"Are they nice?"

Melissa smiled, and her radiance increased. "Heavens are the best."

Honey leaned back out of Melissa's line of sight and shook her head while mouthing the word "no."

"What goes on there?"

"Everyone sits around praising their god all day every day."

"I can wait for the winter solstice."

"OK," said Honey. "So, we were about to go visit my daughter. You can wait here or …"

"You have a daughter?"

"Yes, she is the one ray of sunshine in the hellish nightmare I have made of my life."

Melissa moved to hug Honey, but Honey held her arm out to hold the angel back.

"Wow, you two are just like Louisa and Parnell," Max said, and it's at this time I should explain who Louisa and Parnell are. You see, while it's not completely understood why, it is an inevitability that in every universe in which life occurs at some point an author by the name of T.G. Wills will write a one hundred and twenty-seven book romance series called *The Struggles* about two enemies to lovers named Louisa and Parnell. In universes in which humans don't exist, they are invented by the author as a fantasy race. This has happened in every single universe across the whole cosmos except one. As a result, it is often used as a common reference point among interuniversal travelers. A bunch of memes, if you will, shared by people from every, or rather, nearly every reality. If you're wondering if they're any good, the common consensus is that they're terrible, but also irresistibly addictive.

"I never thought about it before, but you're right we are," Honey said.

"I guess I don't have anything to do in the meantime," the man said with a sigh. "So might as well go with you."

"Great, I'm Honey, and this is Melissa."

"Actually, it's Melicintarifer."

"But you can call her Melissa or Mel to make things easier," Honey whispered.

"My name is Max Stallion." The man took off his helmet to reveal a handsome face with a chiseled jawline and blond hair.

CHAPTER 4

Honey stood waiting at the door of the hotel. "You're sure no one's out there?"

"Yes," said Melissa, "I've double-checked; no one is waiting to attack you."

Honey stepped out of the hotel and someone immediately attacked her. A blast of red bolts flew through the air harmlessly exploding against her. She let out a long sigh as the barrage continued unceasingly. "It's like flies buzzing around my face. Harmless, but so annoying." No one moved as Honey just stood receiving the barrage, tired and worn out from the last two decades and more broadly, her life.

Finally accepting this new aspect of her existence, Honey pulled up a hand in a clawing motion. Purple tendrils emerged in a swarm around the direction of the shooting. A man with dark skin emerged from hiding, dodging the tendrils and firing blasts at them to put them at bay.

The man wore a wide-brimmed hat, bent upward on one side, the top black with white trimming and a bright red bottom. A black short coat with a crimson lining covered a white shirt. His pants were black as well, with red socks and white shoes that moments before were shining white but currently accrued dirt as he dodged around.

"He's doing a lot better than you," Honey said to Max as she increased the number of tendrils emerging from the ground.

Max looked at her, quite unsure what to make of the comment. "I hit you with an entire spaceship's worth of weapons."

"Yeah, but you got taken out with one attack. This guy's got style. His outfit is a lot nicer too."

Max looked down at his yellow spandex with red latex gloves and shoes. "This outfit is designed to survive traveling across universes. Its fibers were woven in once-dead stars and made by the forgotten peoples of burned-out universes."

"OK, but his outfit is fuckable."

The man made a desperate gambit and lunged toward Honey. He dropped one of his blasters and swung a fist toward her face. Honey managed a quick, "Oh no, don't—," before it landed and rebounded in not quite the same shape it was before. He rebounded backward and spun his leg around for a quick blow with his foot, which met the same fate. He fell to the ground, his foot and hand both mangled.

"Damn, that must of hurt." Honey leaned forward toward the man.

He looked up at her, before taking one of his guns and pointing it at himself. Honey sent it flying with a quick flick of her hand. "What the hell, man," she said. "Lose one fight and you're gonna kill yourself."

"I'd rather die than let you take me alive."

"That's pretty hardcore. Not gonna lie; turns me on a little."

"Kill me, like you did my people."

"So, here's the thing …" Honey began putting her hands together.

"You don't know who he is, do you?" Max asked.

"No, I'm sorry. It's like, and I know this sounds terrible, but, and I don't mean it the way it sounds, but from my perspective, you understand, a person doesn't remember every fly they ever swatted, if any. You know you've swatted flies, sure, but they don't stick in your memory longer than it takes to tell someone you killed a fly today."

"Wow," Max said.

"Yeah, ouch," the man on the ground said.

"I'm sorry, I'm so sorry. I'm trying to be better now, and I want to do right by both of you, even though that's impossible, plus I'm still trying to do right here. It's a … it's a long list. So let me fix your foot, and your hand, and you can get in line right behind Max here."

"What did you do to him?" the man asked.

"I committed a near-genocide against his people."

"I'd appreciate it if you stopped calling it a 'near' genocide."

"I would if I could, Max."

"I want to make sure I have this right," the man said. "You want to make up for what you've done?"

"Yeah, I'm not evil anymore and so sorry about, well … me and just everything."

"How do you intend to make up for killing everyone I ever knew when I was just a child?"

"I don't know; I guess sex isn't a good answer." Honey gave a look to Melissa who nodded with encouragement. "But you know, it's on the table if you're interested. In the meantime I'm just doing what I can. Even though I honestly don't know how to go on like this, but I deserve it so … I will."

The man gave Honey a good long stare at that last sentence before speaking. "You can start by fixing my foot and hand."

Honey passed a hand over the affected areas and set them right. "What's your name then?"

"Name's Jack Stallion."

"Oh, are you two …"

"No," Max said. "I've never seen this man before in my life."

"You are?" Jack said.

"Max Stallion."

"That's incredible, what are the odds?"

"It's not that incredible," Honey said. "I once met a man who could fuck himself. Fairy wish gone wrong actually. Everyone knows about djinn, but people forget you got to be careful with fairy wishes too."

"Honey, sweetie," Melissa said. "What are you talking about?"

"I'm just saying, there's lots of crazy stuff out there. Two people with the same last name is hardly worth balking at. Had to pay to see it; that's how he made his living. He asked me to fix him."

"Did you?"

"He wouldn't give me a refund. I don't think it was too much to ask. Good news is we should be safe now. Rule of threes, probably won't get attacked again any time soon."

Honey would be proven wrong about the rule of threes over the course of the next few days. Though, such rules never held as often as people insisted they did.

Melicintarifer might have found Honey first, but others were close behind her, and while those capable of interuniversal, interdimensional, and/or interrealitial travel weren't many, the witch had cut quite a path in her time. So, a small army arrived piece by piece, each trying to kill her in their own way, and each failing. At which point they went through the usual explanation of Honey having forsworn her evil ways and now feeling incredibly sorry and would, in due time, try and make recompense as best she could. Unfortunate, she currently found herself occupied in such a current recompense for the foreseeable future.

One particular revenge involved a large muscular woman with black hair and tan skin wearing only a hide tunic trying to stab the witch for over three hours. The situation wasn't helped when Honey decided to just continue on the road as the woman jabbed with her large, but crude iron sword. It being rather understandable that someone casually walking away from you while you tried to kill them in revenge is a bit upsetting.

After a bit of interrogation, mid-stabbing attempt, Max managed to learn that the woman had sold her soul to a warlock in order to get here. The situation ultimately resolved when Melissa took a quick trip and retrieved the woman's soul, at which point she collapsed sobbing.

"So," Honey asked once the woman stopped crying. "What did I do to you?"

The woman stared up at Honey with hate in her eyes, a look the witch grew accustomed to a long time ago. "You stole my mother's soul."

Honey's eyes grew wide and she slapped the side of her head. "I forgot about all the souls I stole. I need to return those right away."

"Are souls useful to you?" Max asked.

"No."

"Then why?"

"All my friends had souls. Of course they were all demons and devils, but I just wanted to fit in." Honey sighed, long and remorseful. "I-I'm sorry."

She turned to address the crowd of a few hundred. At this point, most had arrived much earlier and were growing exasperated at the number of others showing up. Mostly it contained the usual assortment of fantasy heroes, a disproportionate amount of whom were brown-haired orphans who'd grown up on their uncles' farms, though some had made their way on the streets. A couple of wizards were in the mix, and far too many woman archers. Some knights, of course, and some with unorthodox magical weapons. One idiot had a double-bladed sword.

Of those out of place, one could find a dozen or so people in spandex with capes. Aside from them, a few groups of people in color-coded uniforms who'd summoned giant robots from somewhere to fight Honey. Getting an exact count on how many groups there were proved rather difficult once they intermingled.

It's difficult to say where exactly the anthropological animals in space armor began and ended. While some were clearly of that variety, others were a bit vague on whether they were animals like humans or humans like animals.

The list ends with two men in very heavy space armor, several skull decorations, holding large guns and highly questionable political beliefs. While Honey agreed to send them home, the general assembly agreed that she'd done nothing wrong when she'd enacted her wrath and ruin on their space empires. Before they could be sent home, they'd both end up killing each other over whose space empire was superior to the other. No one missed them.

It's worth noting that the list of demons and devils who showed up over this time period far exceeded the group of heroes. They, however, made their own home and did not join the group. Which divided up between those going home during the summer solstice and those who'd have to wait for winter. The demons and devils did soften the group at least a little toward Honey as she'd clearly done as much if not more harm to the evil creatures of the cosmos during her wilder days.

"OK, everyone, we're going to take a slight detour so I can free some souls."

A few groans and complaints arose.

"Not to worry, we're still going to be able to get the majority of you home during the summer solstice. Our travel plans don't affect the planet's rotation nor its axial tilt."

Several hands went up.

"OK." Honey pinched the top of her nose. "For those of you in pre-astrological societies. The planet actually revolves around the sun, and the seasons—"

Shouts of protest and disbelief sounded out.

"It-it's true. You know what? I don't have time to educate you all on space. If someone is holding a laser sword or a gun ask them to explain it to you. The important thing is, we'll still have you all home on schedule; we're just backtracking a bit. Everybody remember to keep to the buddy system. We don't want anybody to get left behind."

A few hands were raised.

Honey pointed to one of them. "You with the spiky hair and oversized weapon."

"Where are we going?"

The witch's crystal palace remained mostly unchanged. An enormous structure clawing at the sky in pastel hues, mismatched against the blue sky and flower field that grew up around it.

"I like it," Melissa said.

Honey scratched a pattern into a piece of parchment. "Don't lie."

"I'm not; it's got … character. Besides, I can't lie."

"How would you feel if we decided to live there?"

"We don't need to get carried away."

"That's what I thought. Here." Honey handed Melissa the parchment. "Can you burn this into the ground around the palace?"

"Of course, what's it for?"

"It'll make sure the souls trapped inside find their way home when I"—Honey wiped a tear from her eye and sniffed—"destroy it."

"Does it mean a lot to you?" Melissa hugged Honey who did not push her away but leaned into the hug.

"It's probably for the best. It is a symbol of that time I destroyed the world after all, but I put so much work into it. So many closets, so many clothes, so many memories."

"Do you really need many closets when you can make clothes out of anything?"

"That's exactly why I need them. Go." Honey waved Melissa away. "Make the rune."

Melissa flew around the ground of the palace, burning the pattern into the ground with a beam of fire. After she finished, Honey asked for a moment alone with the palace.

"I'm going to miss you," she said, throwing herself against the palace and hugging it as best as someone can hug something several thousand times their size. Pulling away, she placed a hand on the palace and it disintegrated, leaving behind a multicolored cloud that disappeared in the wind.

Honey returned to the group, humming something that suspiciously sounded like "The Way We Were."

"You going to be OK?" Melissa asked.

"I'll be fine; it's closure really, on my past. The last remnant of the person I used to be. Maybe I should have made a thing of it. Invited representatives of nations, but, souls were trapped inside. It's what gave it that"—her voice grew tight and strained to the point of choking up—"extra bit of color."

Melissa tried to hug her again, but Honey held up a hand and walked over to the big muscular woman who'd come to avenge her mother's soul. "Your mother's soul will find its way home soon. I, uh, I'm sorry, about me, that I am me. I wish I was someone else, but … I hope you consider it punishment enough that I have to wake up every day to be me."

The woman cried upon learning her mother's soul would be restored, but said nothing.

CHAPTER 5

Alma and Alteem were staying in a village. Some miners ended up trapped in the mine, and time was running out. Alma tripped over a hole, which turned out to be a cave. The cave led toward the mine, where they found a thin, easily breakable wall that let them rescue the miners in time. The cave also had a rich deposit of iron they could mine much more safely.

As a reward, the villagers gave them a free place to stay, where she'd given the innkeeper's son the courage to confess his love to the richest man in town's daughter. She loved him back, but her father wouldn't consent to the marriage. Then Alma talked to him, and, after a brief conversation, he changed his mind.

The man also happened to be the owner of the mine, and, because of the happiness of his daughter's marriage, he gave a raise to all the miners and let them unionize.

Upon hearing this news, a visiting merchant resolved to reunite with his own son who'd taken up acting. The father hadn't approved of his career and they hadn't seen each other since the son left. That afternoon, an acting troupe arrived in the village, and I'll bet you can guess who just happened to be in that troupe.

The son and father reunited, and the son introduced his boyfriend. After a brief bit of awkwardness the three embraced, a happy family once more.

As the evening wound down and Alma and Alteem ate supper together, all she said was, "Good thing I tripped on that cave, huh?"

"Sure was," Alteem responded.

They arrived in a city next, where Alma happened to spot a glint in the ground. After a bit of digging, she found an emerald necklace and became determined to find the necklace's owner. She spent the better part of the day searching for the owner, but no one claimed it.

In the evening, an old man approached her demanding to know where she got the necklace. The man turned out to be a well-known miser, spending his days working and nights alone. Famous for paying his workers as little as possible, and spending nothing.

The necklace, as it turned out, belonged to a niece of his who died in a fire. Alma returned it, and, upon seeing her generosity in giving up the necklace freely, he decided to abscond from his greedy ways.

He even decided to donate a good portion of his wealth to the local orphanage, and upon doing so, discovered that his niece had not died in the fire. Too young to remember her uncle, she'd been sent to an orphanage by the police who lost track of her and claimed she died. The girl grew up to run the orphanage and the two reunited. He decided to adopt all the orphans, and, upon learning one had a common but deadly illness, donated money to help cure it.

The physician, upon receiving the donation, managed to buy a crucial tool he needed and discovered the cure that very night.

"Good thing I found that necklace, huh?" Alma said.

"Sure was," Alteem responded.

So had been, and so it continued to be, traveling with Alma. Every part of the journey met with unusual good fortune, which chained into yet more good fortune. People reunited, hearts converted, goodwill spread wherever the young girl walked. Sometimes small minor things, other times major shifts in the places they visited.

The girl was, as he initially suspected, a cataclysm of goodness. Where she passed, the goodness sprinkled down, and if she stayed in one place it could flood over. She, herself, acted completely oblivious to the effect she had. For her, this simply is how the world worked. Alteem hadn't seen Honey in a very long time and not once missed her. Now, he desperately wanted to see her again so he could ask some questions.

Even Alteem found he did not feel his sorrows the more time he spent around the girl. His memories of loss and pain turned into memories of happiness for the times he once had with those he loved. Even aware of it, he could not help himself.

They arrived, at last, in Waluigia, where Mathew lived. Alteem kept an eye on Alma as they entered the city, waiting for something to happen. Maybe she'd bump into someone, which would make that person stumble into someone else who'd turn out to be their true love. That love would end a family blood feud that lasted generations and had occasion to take lives. Such a thing happened twice on their journey so far.

Nothing happened, and the girl just wrung her hands. "I'm nervous."

"It'll be OK," Alteem said. "He'll be surprised but he's going to love you. I think it might literally be impossible for people not to."

Alma gave Alteem a nudge. "You're always so nice."

"No, not always." But try as he might, he struggled to remember why he'd ever not been nice to anyone. Perhaps he'd been around the girl too long.

"I hope he does. I know I'm dropping a lot on him. Mom told me so many stories about you guys and I've always wanted to meet you."

"Mathew's a good lad; you'll get along great, I promise."

Alma gave a nervous smile. "Hey, what's that?" she said spotting something in an alleyway.

Alteem hurried her along. "It can probably wait for when we leave." He found himself eager for her to meet Mathew too. He needed to talk to someone else about her and the things that happened around her.

Waluigia was an old city, which is the term used for cities that existed before the witch but weren't fully wiped out by her. Such cities were marked by large sections of houses that at this point had given back over to nature. The once free real estate eventually hit a point where the old buildings wore down enough and no one found it worth the effort to restore them.

Yes, every once in a while some politician or other campaigned on reclaiming these parts of the city. The effort and the cost eventually wore down even those who meant it, and very little progress ever got made.

Such places were often viewed with danger and suspicion and stories of people being lost to specters were abound. In truth, outlaws and gangs often still roamed these places. Those for whom the question of whether the remote but real risk of the building collapsing on you got decided by circumstance.

Mathew's house lay in one of the nicer parts of town, as one might expect from a successful lawyer. They stopped by, but no one was home and Alteem determined it best to return in the evening when working hours would be over.

He took Alma out to eat at a local tavern. "I should tell you," he said after their drinks arrived, "Mathew has a family of his own." The subject should have been brought up earlier, but Alma's strange nature had occupied most of Alteem's attention. Only upon arriving did he remember to bring it up so she'd be prepared.

"Oh," Alma said, taking a drink from a mug of cider. She did not seem troubled at all by the news.

"I just wanted you to be prepared."

"OK."

Alteem lifted his own mug of ale halfway up. "You have a sister and a brother."

"That sounds lovely. I can't wait to meet them."

Alteem didn't know what else he expected. If you've wondered about your missing father your whole life and discover he has a family in the meantime a person should surely react some sort of way about it. Alma, however, remained Alma.

When the lanterns started to light as the sun faded away, they made their journey back to Mathew's house. The gleam of firelight growing stronger as they walked. The glow from the windows of the townhouses helped light the street almost as much as the lanterns.

They arrived; Alma took one deep breath and knocked on the door. Mathew answered, a beard on his face that was starting to show its first signs of gray. He looked first at Alma, the sort of confused expectant look when someone you don't know greets you at your doorway. Seeing Alteem, he smiled. "Alteem, what a surprise." Then his gaze went back to the girl, and a slight flicker of recognition crossed his face. The girl did look a great deal like her grandmother.

"Hello," she said, holding out a hand for a handshake. "I'm so glad to meet you; I'm your daughter."

Alteem laughed, partly because of the awkwardness of it, but also in relief that the girl did at least have some flaw. It didn't surprise him that she'd lack a bit of tact given who'd raised her.

"Wha—," Mathew started but his sentence ended there.

"I should explain," Alma said, talking as if this information were no more important than the weather. Of course, the weather is actually pretty important, especially if you're a farmer. Why do people act so nonchalant about the weather? Maybe it's more about the fact that people feel safe discussing it with each other over other topics than the actual importance of the subject itself.

Anyway, Alteem put a hand on her shoulder. "Mathew, do you remember that time you got drunk with Honeydrops?"

Mathew's face squinted; then he remembered and his eyes went wide. He looked at the girl, putting the pieces together. "Hold on."

"I hadn't thought about it past this part," Alma said.

Alteem gave the girl's shoulder a gentle squeeze. "Don't do much planning?"

"Things have always just worked out for me."

"I've noticed."

Mathew managed to collect himself a bit. He stepped aside and motioned inward. "I think perhaps you two should come in. Alteem, and ..."

41

"Alma."

Mathew's eyes widened at the name. "Right. Head on in and take a seat." He pulled Alteem aside. "Is she ... what is she like?"

He gave the younger man a pat on the arm. "You'll see."

They sat down in the living room. Two couches sat across from each other with dark red upholstery. A rocking chair held an old woman by the fireplace, gray hair, and dressed in an older fashion. Mathew's mother-in-law. His wife, Issa, sat on one of the other three chairs reading a book. Her skin was a shade darker than Mathew's, with long dark hair pulled back in a bun. She wore a green silk dress with ruffles around her neck and watched Alma over her book. A doctor's bag sat beside her chair. Two children, sat playing on the floor, but they got up to greet Alteem, whom they knew.

He fawned over them a moment, but the business of Alma couldn't wait too long so he set them back to their playing. "So, Issa, this is some shocking news."

"Oh," Issa said, putting a finger in her book and placing it on her lap. "What trouble has Alteem brought with him this time?"

"I'm Mathew's daughter," Alma said, her face smiling and bright.

Issa dropped her book, and Alteem had to stifle a laugh. He knew it must be a strange shock to have an unknown daughter of your husband drop in like this, but Alma blurting it out caught him off guard. The woman looked to Mathew, expecting some explanation.

"You remember I told you that before my mother died we went on an adventure with the witch?"

Issa's hand gripped her chair and her knuckles turned white. "You are not saying to me what I think you're saying to me?"

Alteem might have felt some sympathy for a woman to find out her husband had a child with a woman most considered a monster, but he had a suspicion as to what would happen next. He turned out to be right.

"I really didn't mean to trouble you with my arrival," Alma said. She glided over to the woman and took the hand that a moment earlier had clutched the chair. Issa's face softened as soon as Alma touched her hand. "I'm sure this must be upsetting, but my wish is that we can all get to know each other and one day all consider each other family."

And like that, Alma's strange magic went to work. "It would be nice for the children to have an older sister," Issa said.

"I should like that very much, and I hope my presence here can only bring your family more joy, and all our love should be multiplied for it."

Mathew, for his part, looked almost as shocked as his wife was a moment ago. He looked at Alteem who shrugged. This is the way it goes with her, he tried to impart with the gesture.

"Yes, I should like that." Issa stood up and hugged Alma. "Welcome to the family."

Alteem thought he heard a mystified curse under Mathew's breath. "The fuck?"

Alma returned to her seat. "Now that's settled, I'm sure you have lots of questions for me."

Mathew sat across from the girl and stared at her for a time that felt longer than it truly was. "Can you do magic?"

"Of course." Alma pulled out her deck of cards again. "Pick a card, any card."

The kids got excited, but Mathew insisted they could see it another time.

CHAPTER 6

Honey wiped the sweat from her forehead. She'd spent the whole day drawing runes on the hill in preparation for the summer solstice. The attempts on her life had slowed and finally come to an end, for the time at least. The final group to make an attempt on her life being several tiger-like people called Tigerho and the Lightningcats.

"Everything's all set, everyone. Remember, we're on a tight schedule to get you all home. If you've made any friends, say your goodbyes now. Come tomorrow you may not have time for them. I don't want any tearful hugging in front of portals. There are over a thousand of you now, and we need things to be one and done. I open your portal; you go through. Any questions?"

The hand of an androgynous warrior in colorful skimpy armor went up. "I heard you were offering sex in restitution for past wrongs; is that offer still on the table?"

"I ... damn it, Jack, what have you been telling them?"

Jack sat on a rock nearby rolling a coin over his knuckles. "The truth."

Honey paused. "OK, well, it's kind of too late for that. I'm sorry. You know, if we ever meet again, we can get busy. That said, I'm apparently not that good at sex. I mean, I get it, I'm hot; who wouldn't want some? But you'd probably just be disappointed."

"I'm open to it," said the warrior, and a dozen or so others piped up that they'd accept it too.

"I'm gonna be busy all day today and tomorrow so if you wanted sex you should have asked when we had time."

"I didn't know earlier."

"I can't do anything about that. Any other questions? No one? OK, some volunteers are going to give everyone their time card. Make sure you arrive in time for your portal home, and if you can't read, ask someone to read it to you."

Honey sighed and slumped before she walked over to Melissa. "Alright, I just need to fetch my grimoire quick for the next part. I'd hate to ask anyone else for their blood; do you mind?"

"Of course not, Honey." Melissa held out her hand for her.

Max stood nearby. He'd been a de facto leader of the revengers since he arrived first and helped out in setting up the portals. Jack wandered nearby, curious and at least a little suspicious about the witch's ritual.

Honey conjured a knife from the air and carved a thin slice on Melissa's hand. She made runes on the ground from the angel's golden flaming blood. Once complete she pressed the center of the rune. A portal of liquid gold opened up several times larger than the hundreds of times Honey had done this ritual before. The four fell through it before they even had time to recover from their shock.

Everything went bright as warm waves washed over the four. They arrived on a beach of white sand, not quite sure how exactly they'd come to be there.

"Honey, what?" Melissa sputtered.

"It appears angel blood reacts a bit differently than human blood in spells, which, I admit, I should have guessed." Honey cocked her hip and surveyed the area around them.

"You didn't already know that?" Max asked.

"It's not a common commodity, even in my circles."

Melissa dipped an armored foot in the water. "Where are we?"

"The perfect beach, the unmoving tide, the sense of peace and calm, the complete lack of people, the vague presence of an angelic choir humming in the background. I think we're in heaven. Fuck, this is going to screw up the whole schedule."

"Heaven?" Max looked around. "I didn't think it'd be so … physical."

"Which heaven?" Melissa asked.

"I think my universe's. I'm pretty sure I know this beach." Honey scooped up some sand, which fell freely from her fingers. "See this? The sand doesn't stick everywhere. Just goes right back to the beach. Be a great place to have sex if anyone in heaven ever did. Hey, Melissa, how've you been?"

"It's not the time, Honey."

"Aw, come on, these two can wait; it's heaven, there's plenty to do."

"We need to find the god here so we can get out."

Honey let out a troubled hiss. "About that …"

"You didn't."

"On accident."

"How do you accidentally kill the creator of your universe?!"

"I was young and really high. Only time I ever did drugs. Well, that specific combination of drugs."

Jack laughed. "I never stood a chance, did I?"

"I didn't want to hurt your feelings, but no, not even a little." Honey gave him a conciliatory look.

Melissa grabbed Honey by the shoulders. "Tell me what happened?"

"I'm a bit fuzzy on the details. I was with my first boyfriend, and we snuck in to have sex in heaven. It remains an unfulfilled goal. Something, something, something, God died, we replaced him with a scarecrow."

Melissa dropped her hands. "Some important details are missing."

"I don't know, I remember being naked for most of it, but not much else. I think I gave someone a hand job, but I don't know who."

Melissa pinched the bridge of her nose. "Honey, I love you, but I need you to focus here. Why?"

Honey tiptoed away on the beach. Her footprints disappearing not long after they appeared. "We were really high, and I get paranoid when I'm high. I thought we'd get in trouble, so we tried to cover it up. No one noticed."

Max scoffed. "How could no one notice?"

"Most gods are dicks. The dickiest dicks who ever did dick. Narcissistic freaks who make everything about them. Humans can't even look at them without suffering consequences; angels aren't supposed to, and they only communicate through a designated messenger. So, we bribed the messenger to keep quiet and well, nothing else changed."

"Damn."

"Not all gods are bad; Melissa's god is the best."

"The best!" Melissa agreed.

"How so?" Jack decided to attempt to build a sandcastle.

"She bakes." Honey started to wade in the water.

"Bakes?" Max tried burying himself in the sand.

Melissa, as always, got excited talking about her god. Not much about the angel could be described as girly, but when she spoke about her god she had that sort of air about her. "Cookies, cupcakes, doughnuts, pies, pastries, everything."

"No calories either," Honey added as she sat in the water. "High nutritional value. Tastes amazing. She's a decent person, none of that temptation bullshit."

"Good for your teeth too," Melissa added. "Not that I have to worry about any of those things as an angel."

"I even talked her into getting high one time." Honey was picking up handfuls of water and letting them drip through her fingers.

"You what?" Melissa flew over to Honey and hovered above the water.

Jack started laughing and ruined his sandcastle. Max wiggled his feet so they appeared out from the sand.

"You wanna know the best part?" Honey turned to give Max and Jack a sly look and Melissa looked back and forth between them.

"What's that?"

"Melissa got high too and she doesn't remember any of it."

Jack and Max rolled around on the beach laughing.

Melissa grabbed Honey in a panic, her wings dipping into the water and setting it to steam. "What—what did we do? What happened?"

"Oh relax." Honey splashed some water up at her, which sizzled where it landed on her skin. "We spent the whole time making kittens and watching them play. Claire fell asleep and we banged on her bed."

Melissa pushed Honey over into the water. The witch emerged laughing, and pulled Melissa into the water with her. The water around them started to simmer and eventually boil. "I do remember a day we had to find homes for a bunch of very adorable kittens, and you got my god a new bedsheet."

"Things got weird."

"What did you have me do?"

Honey laughed and put her arms around the angel. "What did *you* have *me* do?"

Melissa's eyes got wide and she let out a panicked whisper. "What did I have you do?"

Honey touched her forehead to Melissa's, the witch's wet face drying as the water steamed off her. "You're so cute when I embarrass you. One of the reasons I—"

"Honey, are you OK?" Melissa hadn't wanted to stop Honey, but she sensed the unusual behavior. Desperate as she was to hear what her lover came so close to saying, she didn't want it like this.

Pulling back, Honey got to her feet. "Heaven is getting to us; I need to snap out of it. Max, Jack!" She trudged over to the two who currently occupied themselves making sand angels. "We need to get out of here."

"I wanna stay." Max rolled around in the sand.

"Yeah," said Jack, tossing sand in her direction. "Let us stay."

Honey slapped Max.

"Ow!" Max rubbed his cheek. "Did you have to?"

"No. Now come, we need to get out of here before the sense of peace washes away all our pains and we become happy and content forever."

"You're really not selling me here."

She grabbed Max by his spandex-like clothes and screamed in his face. "It's a fate worse than death!"

"I don't notice anything," Melissa said.

Honey hoisted Max to his feet before grabbing Jack too. "You're an angel; heaven is normal for you. Weird, it never affected me much before."

"You're not evil anymore," Melissa said.

"Huh?" The sound of trumpets appeared in the distance. "They found us, but how?"

Two angels were flying toward them in the distance. The sounds of trumpets growing louder as they approached. The angels had two sets of wings on their backs in the form of an X. The tips of the wings curled inward. On their heads they had bronze circlets that covered where their eyes would be. Over the circlets were etchings of eyes in different shapes that looked around and blinked independently of the others. Their skin looked like liquid metal, one angel gold, the other silver, flowing around them as they moved but otherwise acting solid.

They pointed swords of flowing wind at Melicintarifer when they landed before the group, the trumpets stopping. Each angel stood eight feet tall. "We sensed a divine power not of our gods; what are you doing here?"

Melissa looked at Honey, but the angels ignored the humans. "I came here by accident."

The angels lowered their swords. "Are these three with you? Our god has not ascended a human to heaven in many centuries."

Honey nudged Jack and giggled. "Care to guess why?" He giggled back, but Melissa shushed them.

"Yes, they are. We need a way back to the mortal plane."

The angels were unreadable with their many etched eyes that gave no uniform expression. "We shall take you to our god; he will judge if what you say is true and if he commands, we shall return you to where you came from."

"That's OK." Melissa raised her hands and backed away. "We can find our own way home."

The angels raised their swords again. "You will come with us."

"Honey, do something!"

Honey gave a languid smile. "I kinda want to see what happens." Then she, Jack, and Max fell into giggling fits again.

They followed the angels back to the seat of god, where rows and rows of humans and angels all bowed and sang his praises. The humans' eyes were glossy, and their voices had given out long ago, but still they mouthed the words. Their expressions happy and content.

"I get it now," Max said to Honey.

"Avert your eyes from God," the angels instructed. "Or they will burn out from his glory."

"Yeah, OK," Honey scoffed.

At first, nothing seemed amiss on the throne. Once they got close enough, Melissa could just see bits of straw poking out of the divine figure. Honey made a convincing illusion, but it likely only held because no one dared question their god. An angel with six wings saw them approaching, his circlet and skin gold. Even with their unreadable eyes, he clearly went into a panic on seeing Honey.

"Hello, hello, that's far enough, thus sayeth the Lord," the angel said.

"These intruders say they have arrived by accident and wish to return," the other gold angel informed him.

"Yup, send them home. That's what he says. Go ahead and do it."

The two angels turned their heads slightly toward each other and back to the gold angel. "Only God has the power to open the gateway of heaven."

51

"Right, ummm, well, they can see themselves home. Just get them what they need. Th-thus sayeth the Lord."

One of the angels tilted their head to god, and after an examination, flew closer.

"God says back off," the gold angel said in a panic.

The angel who approached the scarecrow god got close, and then pulled a piece of straw through god's robes. "What trickery is this?" She slashed her sword through the false god and straw poured forth. The scarecrow collapsed and the illusion broke, turning into a pile of straw in a tattered gray robe with a rotted pumpkin head resting on the throne of god.

People did not take it well. The angels swarmed like a hornet's nest, Honey, Melissa, Jack, and Max fleeing. The humans tried to scream out in agony, but their voices were gone so hundreds of thousands of people's faces turned into silent screams. The golden angel hastily tried to restore god, but all he did was fluff up the straw. Once their silent scream ended, some fled, while others charged the throne of god, their mouths working wordlessly.

The chase didn't last long, thousands of angels versus the group of four and not much of heaven to hide in. Melissa conjured her molten sword, Max drew his ray gun, and Jack his two plasma guns.

"Honey, now would be a great time for some of that all-powerful magic of yours."

Honey hesitated. "I don't really wanna kill a bunch of angels; I have enough on my conscience. Mass murder is something I prefer to avoid these days."

"Do something!"

Shrugging, Honey flexed her hands and raised them up. Purple tentacles emerged from the ground of heaven, and started to grab the angels from the air. Even as it captured hundreds of them, thousands more descended.

Melissa went into combat, dancing like fire, beating back the angels even as they outnumbered her. Max and Jack supported her with their guns; not powerful enough to kill the angels, they stunned them and helped keep them off Melissa's back. Honey continued her work, but even as the ground became littered with trapped angels, more poured forth, and Melissa started to lose ground.

"Honey, I can't use divine power against angels; it won't hurt them. I need you to do something."

"This better not work!" Honey shouted. She raised her hand up, muttered some dark words and the angels around Melissa were blasted away. She grabbed Melissa, spun her around and kissed her. With one hand, she traced a circle in the air, and a portal opened.

"You did it! You opened a way out of heaven!" Melissa shouted.

"What is wrong with you, Melissa?" Honey said.

Jack and Max wasted no time in diving through the portal. Melissa stared at Honey, confused by the question. She grabbed the witch and escaped from heaven.

CHAPTER 7

They shot out of heaven into a jungle. Rain poured down, sizzling on Melissa's skin and wings. Max fell to the ground screaming, Jack collapsed and clawed at the earth, and Honey took a few staggering steps before collapsing onto her knees.

"What's wrong?" Melissa went to Honey's side and held on to her arms.

Through groans and screams Honey answered, "Coming out of heaven is not good for humans. I've never felt it this bad."

"I can't." Jack took one of his guns and pointed it at his head but Honey knocked it away with a casual blast of purple energy.

"It'll pass," Honey said. "It just takes a few days."

Max pulled at his own hair. "Days?!"

"Maybe longer, since it's worse than usual."

Melissa folded a wing around Honey and held her close.

"Oh." Honey clung to the angel and started to press her hands against her skin. "That's nice; your divine radiance helps."

Jack crawled over. "Please." He reached for the angel.

"You can't." Honey dove on him to stop him. "She'll burn you alive if you touch her bare skin."

"It's better than this." Jack tried to free himself from Honey, squirming beneath her grip.

"I have an idea; it might not work." Honey took the hands of Jack and Max. A purple glow encased them all. Once the glow faded, Honey collapsed into a writhing, twisting fit on the ground. Her body shivered and sweat mixed with the rain.

Max stood up, examining his hands. "It's gone; what did she do?"

Jack stood a bit slower, massaging parts of his body.

Melissa swept Honey up into her arms, wrapping herself around the witch. Honey stopped twisting as much, but she remained shivering and sweating. A whimper sometimes escaping from her. Her eyes closed. "I think she took your pain onto herself."

"No, she didn't need to do that." Max put a hand on Honey's forehead, but she responded to nothing. "Can't you do something?"

Melissa looked around them. "I am no healer. We must figure out where we are."

"I'm not native to this planet," Max said.

"None of us are." Jack looked about. The rain poured in around them, already rising. "Shelter is usually the first priority in these scenarios. Maybe you don't need it, angel, but it will give us a place to regroup and come up with a plan."

Melissa stretched one of her wings to provide cover from the rain for her companions. She carried Honey in her arms and wrapped her other wing around the witch. "Let us find somewhere, then."

They trudged through the jungle, a burning flame in the sea of green and rising rain. Wandering blind, they made their way through the trees and foliage. Humans under such circumstances would have wandered in circles, but Melissa had no such problem. She marched on, summoning her flaming sword and hacking through the jungle when needed. Even so, they had no destination, and no idea what they might find.

Honey remained limp in her arms, not speaking and her only movement her constant tremble.

The rain around them stopped, like an invisible dome had appeared around them. When I say "like," I mean, it did; an invisible dome appeared around them. Ahead appeared a man. His skin a dark brown, and on his head, a crown of blue feathers at least a foot long pointed upward. On his face was black paint with blue swirls among it, and his eyes glowed amber. He wore an elaborate robe, with arcane swirls of copper on a dark background cinched just below his chest. His chest had more black paint, with gold chains and turquoise jewels dangling down from it. Gold bracelets were on his wrist and from them hung a rainbow of feathers. In his hand the apparent source of the invisible dome, a stick of redwood. A gold mask hung from a beaded chain on one end and from the other a leather cord with several shining stones.

His voice came through calm and soft. "I thought I sensed something come through one of the other places, but this I did not expect."

"We need help," Melissa said, stepping forward and unfurling her wing. "She's hurt."

The man came forward to look at Honey. "We will always help those in—oh, it's her."

Melissa looked down at Honey's pained face. "You know her?"

"She killed all the members of my coven, leaving only me as a survivor. I've been rebuilding these past two decades."

Melissa fell to her knees. "Please, she's in so much pain. I know she's done terrible things in the past, but she's different now."

"Fear not," the man said. "I am sworn to help all those in need, even this bitch. Call me Talcune; let me have a look at her." Talcune examined Honey, lifting up her eyelids where her eyes shone bloodshot and wild. "I never thought anything could hurt her. What happened?"

"We were in heaven, and it affected them." Melissa stroked Honey's face and the witch let out a moan.

"When we came back she took our pain on her so now she's feeling all of it," Max finished.

Talcune gave a troubled sigh. "Energies from the other places are not in any power of mine to heal. We can beseech the spirits of the earth on her behalf, but I do not know if they would help her."

"Because of what she has done?"

57

Talcune made a half gesture of affirmation with his hand. "She has changed, but has she changed enough? We will see." He motioned for them to follow with his staff, the invisible dome around them swaying as the rain sloshed over it. "You three do not seem of this world."

"I'm Jack Stallion; this is Max Stallion, no relation. This is Melissa." He leaned over and whispered. "She's an angel."

"Usually if someone from other places comes to our world, it has to do with her."

"We tried to kill her," Jack said.

"It did not work," Max said.

"Not even a little." Jack twirled one of his guns in his hand. "Tough little cookie."

"She once cried for half a day when we forgot her birthday, or more accurately didn't know about her birthday because she didn't tell us when it was." Talcune took the opportunity to look over at Honey. "I still remember the young girl who came to learn from our coven. Terrifying in her power even then."

The man led them to a place with several huts on stilts. Their sides were made of river reeds and their ceilings of packed straw. About a dozen or so younger men and women moved between them, carrying things, dressed in a manner similar to Talcune but less ornate.

"Elatin!" Talcune called and the eldest of them came running over. "We must prepare for a ceremony of Ashantar; tell the others."

Elatin nodded and ran off.

"Ashantar?" Jack asked.

"It is our name for this world and the spirits who live in it."

Melissa looked around as the apprentices went to work. Some, setting up sticks that warded off the rain and water, began to dig a careful hole in the earth.

"We must prepare her body and in doing so, her soul," Talcune said, and they followed him into the largest hut, where a stone table sat in the middle. Many different dyes had stained the table over its centuries of use, but the most prominent colors were bright reds and greens. Melissa crouched low and maneuvered with care to avoid setting anything on fire with herself. "Set her on the table, strip her, and we shall get to work."

"If I am not touching her, the pain will grow worse." Melissa's eyes were watching Honey's face.

Talcune nodded. "That makes sense; you are an outsider, and a powerful one from what I can sense. We can work around you, but it will be slower."

"She will not sit still if the pain is too great."

Another nod, and Melissa carefully laid Honey onto the table. She took off the witch's clothes, keeping a wing wrapped around her leg or arm at all times. Two apprentices arrived and began drawing on Honey with their fingers, creating different swirly patterns that invoked animals.

Elatin arrived. "I thought perhaps a feather from the outsider's wing could help with the draft."

Melissa flexed one of her wings, its flames roaring briefly. "I would gladly give them all, but I do not know if you have any craft here that can tame one of my feathers."

Elatin laughed and held up a cloth web held in a circle of wood. "This is a spirit web; it is made to hold powerful energies of beings not native to our land. If anything can hold a feather of yours, this will."

"Are you sure of this?" Talcune asked. "If you are careless and touch the feather it will burn more than your hand."

"For her, of course." Elatin looked at Honey with fondness.

Talcune shook his head. "I do not understand you younger folk; go ahead then."

Melissa plucked a feather from her wings, which sputtered and shot sparks to the ground where they left burn marks. She placed the feather into the web where it sat and Elatin walked off with it.

When they finished marking Honey with their runes, two other apprentices arrived with bandages soaked in a white poultice. They placed the strips of cloth around Honey until only her mouth and nose remained visible. Melissa kept her fingers in place on Honey's lips so she remained still.

Elatin returned, a cup in his hands with a flaming gold liquid in it. He anointed the body with the liquid, and told Melissa to smear some across her lips. The liquid continued to burn, but the bandages remained unharmed. "It is finished."

"What next?" Melissa asked.

"We will take her outside, place her in the burrow, and dance and sing to the spirits to beseech their aid."

"Will they help her?"

"I think they will." Elatin put the empty cup away. "She forced those who invaded our land to leave. They cut down our forests and killed our people, but she returned it to us. The forest and the land are healing because of what she did."

"She also poisoned the whole of the world," Talcune added. "I cannot say with any certainty what the spirits will do. We must carry her outside."

Melissa winced in pain, but pulled her fingers away from Honey. The moment contact broke Honey began to writhe and twist in place. Her body straining so badly that it stretched to the point of breaking. The apprentices grabbed her and carried her out to the burrow, which they'd shaped to look like an animal of many different parts. They put her in the center where the twisting continued. Even Talcune, who had every reason to want her suffering, looked away in pity.

They began a rhythmic, chanting dance and song, moving in a circle around the burrow through the night. Melissa and Max watched the witch, as she twitched and turned in the mud. The rain stopped sometime in the dark and the moon came out. When its light shone on the dancing figures, Honey arched upward and screamed. She fell back into the mud, still shivering and unresponsive but no longer twisting and turning.

"The spirits have taken some of her burden," Talcune said.

"But not all of it." Elatin stepped into the pit and placed a hand on the shivering witch. "We could take the rest; if we split it between us it would not be so bad."

"I cannot ask that of you." Melissa stepped into the mud where she placed a hand on Honey's cheek, the bandages there turning to ash. She stopped shivering and fell into a troubled sleep. "I can be with her for as long as needed."

Talcune shook his head once more. "If any of you wish to split this burden among you, that is your choice. I do not approve, but I will not stop you."

"Who will?" Elatin asked. "Even in several ways it will not be easy, but the more who come the easier it will be."

Eight volunteered, plus Max who also volunteered making nine. Some of the burden would remain with Honey for a total of a ten-way split. Melissa would have taken it all, but if such a thing were possible they did not possess the craft. So they placed their hands on Honey, Melissa stepping aside once more to watch as they chanted over her.

The chant grew louder, until lightning struck the body and sent those touching it flying back. Each got to their feet, a mix of groans and careful movements.

Honey stirred, let out a loud curse, and sat up. She looked around, her eyes wide, and she spotted Talcune. "Talcune? Is that you? Did you … help me?" He made a rude gesture at her and disappeared into one of the huts. "I deserved that." She tried to stand, but stumbled and fell into the mud. "I might not be at full strength yet."

Melissa rushed over to the witch and picked her up in her arms. "You're OK." The angel cried and hugged Honey, the bandages burning in her embrace.

Even with the comfort of the divine radiance, Honey pushed herself out of Melissa's arms. Her gaze looking away from the angel. She couldn't quite push away completely since she needed help to stand. "What happened to my clothes?"

"I shall fetch them for you," Elatin said, and brought the witch her dress so she could put something on besides burning bandages.

"How long has it been?"

"A little less than a day." Max rolled his shoulders as if something painful were wedged between them.

61

"How? I should have been out of it for months at least."

Elatin and the others started to smooth the ground over around the burrow. "We split the burden among several of us so that it would be bearable."

"What?!" Honey tried to step toward them, but stumbled and fell back to Melissa. "I took it upon myself because I deserved it. It was my responsibility and my fault it happened."

"I have always wanted to thank you for all you have done for our people." Elatin walked closer to Honey, though his steps were uneasy.

"Do you know all I have done to your people?" Honey glanced around as if looking for the ghosts she'd left there once upon a time.

"Yes, you were wicked once, but you have forced out those who colonized our lands, and helped us heal our forest. You are not the evil you once were, and we recognize the goodness in you now."

Honey leaned toward Melissa and whispered, "Is he insane?"

Melissa just hugged Honey in response. "I was so worried."

"It's fine." Elatin wiped the mud off his hands. "Between the ten of us, it should only last a week at most, maybe only a few days. Your strength may take longer to recover."

"Max? You too?"

Max nodded and rubbed his head. "Not bad as it was when it first hit."

"I don't understand."

Max put a hand on her shoulder. "I like you."

"No you don't. I … killed all your people."

"You're fun, and not the person I expected. It takes a great deal of courage to admit our failings and try to do right by them. I don't know if you can, but, I admire your efforts."

Honey blinked her eyes to avoid tears, and turned away from them. "You're all idiots."

CHAPTER 8

Honey sat alone, watching as the apprentices went about their work. They'd made a crutch for her so she could get around on her own. Melissa pestered her a few times about how exactly they'd gotten out of heaven, but Honey refused to answer.

Max sat down beside her and handed her a yellow fruit as he bit into one of his own.

"How are you like this?" Honey asked him.

"Sorry?"

"I killed everyone in your life, your whole people. I've done that a few times and people don't come out of it as forgiving as you are."

Max cocked his head back and laughed. "Yes, it's hard. Many a time I feel the pain of it all. A man I respected once told me people have two options when something terrible happens to them. They can use it as an excuse to be terrible to others, or they can use it as an excuse to never be terrible to others. I miss those I've lost, but I choose to honor them with the time I have. I am the last of my people and I want our final legacy to be one of goodness. I do still have a lot of questions; why did you renounce evil?"

"Selfishness."

"That's an odd reason to give up evil."

Honey hugged herself. "It's the truth. I did it because I thought it would benefit me. I spent a long time rebelling against what my mother wanted, doing anything and everything to avoid going home and fulfilling our family destiny. Things just got worse and worse, so I finally decided to go home and do what my mother wanted. For a brief time it felt like I finally got my shit together, but then everything fell apart all over again. So, I tried a third path, hoping something completely different would make me happy. Things fell apart again. Then I realized, I'm the problem; it's just me. No matter what I do I mess everything up."

"I don't think that's true." Max scratched the back of his head. "We can fail many times, but that doesn't mean there's something wrong with us. You might have started out for selfish reasons, but you continue for the right ones. Have you never asked why, even after it failed to make you happy, you continued being good?"

Honey cocked her head to the side. "There are still times I want to give up. Not because I want to be evil again, but because I don't think I deserve to be good. Whenever someone thanks me, or tells me how much I've helped, it … hurts. I know I don't deserve it, and I can't let myself believe otherwise."

"You're not so bad."

Honey looked away. "Yes I am; I always will be. I've done far too much."

"Maybe so, maybe not. Who can ever say? I came here for revenge, but I didn't find the person I looked for. I found you, a good person."

"I thought being good would make me happy. That's the only reason I did it. My life was miserable then; it's miserable now."

"Is it so much? Things don't look so bad for you to me. You've an angel who loves you. People in the world who care about you. Maybe things aren't as bad as they seem."

Honey shook her head. "I'll fuck it up somehow; I always do. No one wants to stay around me for long. I don't blame them; I'd get away from myself too if I could. Even if everything got better I don't think I can be happy anymore, knowing I don't deserve it." Honey blinked and tears fell down her cheeks. "All that lies ahead for me is misery and that's the way it should be."

Max put an arm around her shoulder and hugged her. "Punishment doesn't make things right. It just makes more suffering. I came wanting to stop that suffering, thinking that stopping you would be what did it. Now I know better. You've got a lot of work ahead of you. Guess what? Everyone does. Things get worse and things get better. Some days are hard and some days are harder. That doesn't mean all comes to misery."

"I've forgotten how not to be miserable or maybe I never knew how to be anything else. Sorry, you shouldn't have to listen to me whine."

"I don't mind; I like making other people feel better. Talking helps when it's to someone who listens. Was there really never a moment you were happy?"

Honey said nothing at first, watching the wind. "I spent centuries trying to drown the pain with pleasure, mistaking it for joy. So much wasted time in my life, all those years gone. What I wouldn't give to take it back, to know without having to learn. The tapestry of suffering I wove is too complex and big to unwind. The thread runs through me, and binds my heart so tight there isn't a moment I'm not bleeding. To numb myself to the pain is to numb myself to life, and that is even worse."

"I understand that."

"But I'm the one who made your life that way; I created your pain. Why can't you just hate me?"

Max stretched out and took another bite of his fruit. "What good does hate do us? It's intoxicating, hate and anger, the thirst for punishment in vengeance. It's no great crime, of course, to be angry or to hate. There are good reasons to do these things at times, but they can drown us until that's all we know how to feel. It's far too easy to become addicted to our own emotions, even the ones that aren't healthy for us. I won't waste time hating you, so don't try and make me. I don't believe you deserve it either."

Honey turned away from him. "It's all I deserve. I don't even remember what I did to you. That's how much bad stuff I've done. There are crimes against humanity that don't even register because of the sheer quantity."

"You have a lot to make up for; I don't deny that, but you don't have to suffer every moment you do so. Yes, healing hurts at times, but the point of it is to feel better."

"Some things can't be healed, and I accept now that I'm one of them."

"We all have things inside of us that will never heal. Don't think you're special. You wouldn't think a person stricken with a chronic illness is undeserving, would you?"

"No," Honey admitted.

"We are born flailing and crying to life. Of course we make mistakes in trying to figure out life, and we all fall short of who we wish we were. It's such a disservice to ourselves. To imagine our own perfect version of our lives, then to hate ourselves for not being able to do the impossible. You'll never get everyone's forgiveness, but in time perhaps you can earn your own."

"But I don't want to forgive myself. How can I?"

"Perhaps, in time, even that can change. In the meantime there is at least one ready to forgive you, if you'd let them."

"I appreciate it but, you really don't have to."

"I meant Melissa."

"Oooh." Honey curled up and hugged her knees. "She deserves better; I want her to have better."

"It's a dangerous game deciding who should love whom, what would make others happy. You're what she wants, and not for nothing but I did piece together how you got us out of heaven."

"We just hurt each other."

"Yes ... but no. Of course people hurt each other, that's going to happen, but it doesn't have to be just hurting each other. We seek out others because for all the pain of connection, there's far more joy to be found. You made bad choices in the past; you can make different ones now. If you walk a different path, you find a different destination."

"I have trouble walking these days." Honey tapped her crutch.

"Now you're just being difficult."

"No, I think I've been difficult this whole conversation."

"Alright, you can sit here and feel bad for yourself, but I need to go do my midmorning workout."

"I thought I saw you working out already this morning."

"That was more early morning workout; I do three workouts every morning. Early, mid, late. Then of course there's a pre-lunch cooldown and afternoon cardio."

"Alright, well, you know, fuck you."

Max let out a boisterous laugh. "People always say that. You're welcome to join me, do some physical therapy to get your strength back."

"My preferred workout is wild and rough sex."

"Suit yourself." Max squat-thrusted away. "Think about what I said."

Honey sat by herself again, this time trying not to think about what Max said. Try as she might, she thought about it. Eventually, she gave a choked groan and got to her feet to hobble about, looking for Melissa.

She found her helping out the apprentices with their practice. Having an angel to study made for a rare occurrence. Their powers were so like magic and yet so utterly different.

Watching for a while, Honey built up the courage to walk over and start the conversation she'd been avoiding while desperately hoping it would somehow happen. She didn't have to move at all; when Melissa spotted her, the angel smiled and walked over, her wings leaving steaming trails on the wet ground behind.

"How are you?" Melissa asked.

"I'll say one thing. Now that I'm a good person I'm never going back to heaven."

"Honey, that's not really how it—," Melissa started, but stopped. "I'm just glad you're OK."

"Can we, um, talk, about us?"

"Of course." Melissa sounded both excited and nervous for the talk she'd been trying to have for a long time but also never managed to say quite what she wanted to.

"Somewhere private."

"If you'll allow me." Melissa reached for Honey, who nodded. The angel took her lover in her hands and with a single powerful flap of her wings sent them flying into the air as waves of heat rolled over the ground beneath them.

They flew for a while, until Melissa set them down next to a jungle spring. A few nearby animals fleeing at their arrival.

"So?" Melissa said.

"So." Honey tapped at the dirt with her crutch.

"You wanted to talk."

"Yes," Honey said, and they both stood there for what turned out to be around ten seconds though it felt like several minutes to both of them. "You're going to leave me again; you always do."

"I'm not. How many times do I have to—"

"Just, I …" Honey sighed, and took a moment before speaking. "I can't stop feeling like you're going to leave me again."

"I'm not; I promise, things are different this time. You're not evil anymore."

"I'm still me." Honey started to cry, which she knew was an inevitability in the conversation but hadn't expected it quite so early. "I'll fuck it up somehow; I always do. I know you think it'll be different this time, but I'm always going to be me."

"But, it's you that I love."

"Why? What is wrong with you? Why do you love me?"

Melissa smiled, hugged Honey, and breathed a sigh of relief when Honey pressed back against her instead of pulling away. "You always say I don't love you, but you didn't this time."

"True love's kiss. That's how it got us out of heaven. I harnessed the magic of true love's kiss."

Melissa pulled out of the hug slightly and stroked Honey's hair back. "So, you love me too."

Honey pressed her head against Melissa's chest. "Of course I love you, idiot. You're a perfect angel. Seriously, even your ass is perfect."

"OK."

"No, I mean it. The first time I saw it I went blind for half a second; that's how perfect it is."

"Thank you."

"It's really just so amazing."

Melissa pulled back, but kept Honey in her arms. "If you love me, then why are you always pulling away?"

"I'm the worst thing that's ever happened to you. You had the perfect life before I showed up and ruined everything. I don't understand how you could love me."

"You're the best thing that ever happened to me."

"I know that as an angel of goodness you can't lie, but there's no way that's true."

Melissa pulled away and stepped into the spring where the water started to steam and then boil. "Look at me, Honey."

Honey looked at her. "OK yeah, you're hot and sexy as always. Why am I looking?"

"Claire, as much as I love her, made me for a single purpose. She forged me to win a war and did not think of what might happen to me after. I can't touch things without destroying them. My wings are powerful enough to destroy armies, but I can barely fit into someone's home without risking burning it down. I spent millennia watching over the perfect paradise that I helped make, but I wasn't a part of it. Then you appeared in my life and showed me something more wonderful than I ever dreamed."

"Lesbianism?"

"No, idiot, well, yes, but not just that. A world outside the one I knew. I've been across universes and through dimensions because of you. I've found places where I fit in, and then there's you." Melissa reached out and pulled Honey into the spring with her. "Someone I can touch and who touches me back. You never cared that I'm an angel; you just saw someone beautiful whom you loved. Even if it took you way too long to admit."

"Sorry."

"It's OK, because this time, we'll make it work. You're different now, and you inspire me."

"Fuck off, no I don't."

Melissa could not help but laugh, and she pressed her forehead to Honey's. "You do; I never could have changed so much if not for you. I'm more than an angel because of you. So you better start accepting that I love you, because I'm never going to stop. And this time, I'm here to stay, because you've become the person I always knew you could be. Whatever your past, great things lie in your future."

Honey wiped some tears from her eyes. "I never imagined I'd ever done anything good in my life. This whole time I thought I'd only made things worse for you. I'm so relieved to hear that's not true. Also, if we're going to really give this a try I want you to be open about your sexual desires. I need to up my stats."

"We could start now."

"You know me; I'm always ready to go."

"I think I'd like to try your suggestion of being the top for a change." Melissa pushed Honey on her back at the edge of spring, and Honey readily indulged as the water continued to boil around them.

CHAPTER 9

The city of Waluigia hadn't changed much physically in the past few weeks since Alma's arrival, but, well, it all started when she found a lost love letter. Hidden in the previously undiscovered secret compartment of Mathew's home desk. Alma leaned against it when the two were talking and just so happened to press her fingers in quite the right way to open the compartment.

Mathew knew the owner of the letter, having purchased the desk from the very man. Palo Chanez occupied the position of a prosecutor in the city and earned quite the reputation. Scarce was the criminal—or in many cases innocent person—who escaped justice, or often injustice as the case may be, when they assigned Palo the case. Court cases were so often about a good show and less about innocence or guilt.

Upon giving the letter to Palo, he explained he'd written it for the one and only woman he ever loved, Gisela, but never had the nerve to send it. You see, his father didn't approve of the union since he saw the woman as below their station. Palo gave in to his father but always regretted it.

After making inquiries, they discovered that Gisela had a child by Palo. Being an unwed mother at the time of the witch led her to take desperate action and she ended up in prison after stealing some bread. Tragically she died there.

Her son, Edwardo, ended up being raised by a gang of criminals and would even one day become their leader. Palo had, as it turns out, been trying to build a case against Edwardo for some months now. This new information was, to say the least, a bit shocking.

Palo remained divided on whether to contact Edwardo with this information, but Alma, being her, took it upon herself to waltz into the gang leader's territory and speak with him. Such an action would be unquestionably foolhardy for anyone, exceptions being unspeakably powerful beings, and Alma.

A bit of persuading on both sides and Alma facilitated a meeting between the two parties. Initially terse, some prodding and therapy from Alma had the two in a tearful embrace before long.

Learning of each other and the lives they'd lived led to some introspection on each other's parts. Palo, for his part, ended his career as a prosecutor and became an activist for criminal justice reform. Edwardo decided that organizing people to uplift his neighborhood rather than crime would ultimately be a better life lived. Of course, persuading gang members to do the right thing is difficult. Persuading politicians—who are often worse criminals with fewer consequences—to do anything that doesn't benefit them directly is an even more monumental task. But with Alma's help, they managed.

Over the course of the weeks Alma stayed in the city, a transformation took place. Justice changed from punitive to restorative, and criminals everywhere embraced this change. The goodness that had so transformed Mathew's hometown now worked on the city. People became friendly, kinder, and more open. Favors came easier, debts were lifted, and people even stopped locking their doors.

Mathew and Alteem shared a conversation one evening that went, "So."

"So."

"Is this …"

"Yup, everywhere we went."

"Do you …"

"Not a clue."

"It's got to be …"

"Magic? Probably."

And that was all they spoke of the matter for the time being. As for the matter of magic, Alma's half-siblings enjoyed her card tricks. Mathew fully endorsed their enthusiasm, but only half-listened to their descriptions.

Thusly, life continued in the city; families reunited, orphans found homes, people found their lost pets. There isn't really a city equivalent to the idyllic small town, so I don't have as apt a comparison. Small towns are allowed to be idyllic in fiction; cites are not, because they are well known for being places where no one talks to each other because they're too busy committing all the crimes. This isn't true; it never has been. People love their cities, and communities form there just as they do anywhere else. Yes, we need to pretend otherwise to make people in small towns feel better about the fact they don't get big concerts or traveling musicals without having to drive for a long distance. Yes you can go down to the local bar and hear a band do a half-decent cover of "Fat Bottomed Girls," but it's just not the same. Cities are allowed to be utopias in fiction, but only if there's something sinister behind it. Though, to be fair, this is often true of small towns as well.

Where were we? Ah, yes, after Alma spent a couple of weeks in the city, a fleet of spaceships appeared overhead.

It's safe to say that an unexpected fleet of spaceships is rarely the sort of thing a person wants to see appear in the sky overhead. This is doubly true if you have no idea what a spaceship is. A mixture of panic and panicked curiosity swept over the city.

The spaceships were large, imposing rectangular prism things with sextets of engines on their rear. The sides of the ship had a red triangle emblem with a black hawk. Varying in size from big to gigantic, it's safe to say if we had a soundtrack some seriously ominous music would start playing about now. Maybe starting with one of those "bwam" noises that have become so popular in movie trailers. I looked it up and it's called a BRAAAM.

Hundreds of black boxes launched from the ships. They hurled to the ground causing the city to shake with the impact of so many. The lids of the boxes fell away with a hiss and they emerged.

Humanoid shapes of gray metal with shiny doll-like limbs. Their heads were round, but for the large visors that covered their faces. The visors extended down from the forehead to below the chin. With a semitranslucent green tint, in the light one could just make out the hint of the faces beneath. It was impossible to glean any hint that the faces were alive, but they were.

Batons in their hands, and coiled guns at their hips, they started to round up the people of the city. Those who resisted received the baton, and those who persisted received worse.

Once the panic had mostly subsided and the people outside were gathered in crowds watched by the beings, beams of green cones shot out of the ships. Where they hit appeared men and women who wore gray military uniforms. Pentagonal hats adorned their heads with the red triangle and black hawk adoring them. The emblem also adorned the left crest of their chests with different colored stripes and dots below. Black boots covered their feet, and black gloves held up a picture of a girl, Alma.

"We have come here to apprehend someone of interest to our organization. Those who cooperate will recieve no harm," they said. Questions were asked, but most people received the baton regardless of their level of cooperation. Authoritarians aren't known for their trusting natures, so even if you tell them the truth, they're still gonna hurt you.

The questioning eventually pointed them toward a particular house. Commander Nitrel marched down toward this house with a complement of the doll troops and their living death masks beneath the visors. Two other officers flanked him. Nitrel himself, had shiny black hair—too shiny really, as he put too much product in it. Especially since it started turning gray. Pallid skin with a face shaven clean showed off the sharp jaw, which was contrasted by the shallow cheekbones. Despite being above average height, he wore heels to seem even taller, but of his many terrible qualities, let's not hold this against him.

He pounded on the door with a black-gloved fist.

Alteem answered, an unnecessary cane in his hand. "May I help you, sir?" His eyes passed over the people behind the man.

"We are searching for an individual and have been informed she may be on these premises." The man held up a picture.

Alteem did not look at the picture; he did not need to. Word spread quickly about who the invaders were looking for. Instead, he scanned the entourage before him. "And who might you be?"

"I am Commander Nitrel of the Cosmos Guardians. Do you recognize the person in the picture?"

Alteem continued to ignore the picture. Instead squinting at nothing. "You'll forgive me; my eyes aren't what they used to be. May I ask what gives you the right to disrupt people's lives like this?"

"The Counsel of Omungal." The man brought the picture closer to Alteem. "The picture, sir?"

"Never heard of them." Alteem did not look at the picture.

"They created the Cosmos Guardians to hunt and either imprison or eliminate criminals dangerous to the cosmos. It is better you cooperate, sir."

"So, they created you and then gave you authority to act like this. Who gave them the authority?"

Nitrel's face tightened; he pocketed the picture, made a motion with his hands and pushed Alteem out of the way. The old teacher stumbled back and crashed into the wall, despite Nitrel not having seemed to use much effort.

The group stormed into the house where they began ransacking the place. They broke open anything locked, cut open pillows and cushions, broke apart furniture.

Alteem recovered and walked after the man. "This person of interest must be quite remarkable if they can hide inside cushions."

"Standard procedure I assure you," Nitrel said without looking at him. One of the officers came up to Nitrel; she held a small device in her hand with a black screen on it.

"They've not located the target, sir, but sensors detect footprints heading out the back way."

"There's no evading the Cosmos Guardians," Nitrel said to Alteem. "You can make this easier, but we'll catch them either way. The question is what will happen in the meantime?"

"I've no idea what you mean, sir," Alteem responded.

"Take him," Nitrel said, and the officer pressed some things on her screen. The metal doll soldiers took Alteem who gave no struggle.

"I think maybe you don't quite understand who you're hunting," Alteem said with the hint of a threat in his voice.

"We understand, and we've made every preparation. The witch will fall at last, and her reign of terror will end. I thought the people of this world would aid in her end."

"Seems your preparation isn't as complete as you thought. Things change; people change. Maybe you should rethink some things because this isn't going to end how you think it will."

"Let me know if you find them," Nitrel said to his officer. "I've an interrogation to conduct."

"You can if you really have to." Alteem gave a shrug and smile. "But I've been tortured by the best. I'm quite numb to it by now. You'll really just be wasting your time."

CHAPTER 10

Honey, Melissa, Max, and Jack sat by a fire.

"Well, Melissa can't fly us, without killing you guys, so the only option is by ship, which would take months to cross the ocean. Unless we travel by way of hell, and honestly after heaven I'm not keen on any other such incursions." Honey still had her crutch, though she didn't need it quite as much as the days went by.

"You're a witch," said Jack. "Can't you make flying brooms?"

"Flying brooms?"

"Yeah, it's a witch thing; you put it between your legs and fly on it."

Honey stared at him with her eyebrows creeping upward. "You want to put all our weight on a thin piece of wood wedged into our crotch?"

"I never thought about it quite like that. Doesn't make much sense as a way of flying, does it?"

"You have some weird ideas about witches."

"It's a common cliché where I come from."

"That's even weirder." Honey rested her hand on her chin. "The idea of making something to fly on isn't the worst idea. We'd need something more practical than a broom. Best to be in a chamber, since even with magic we'd fly a while. To keep it aerodynamic it should be like a tube with a gradual nose-like point in the front. Maintaining the magic to keep it aloft the whole time would be a pain, so, we could just attach a propeller to the front and I could power that by magic.

Throwing some wings on the side so it can glide in the air would make it require even less magic. Then we add a tail with some fins on the back to help stabilize it."

"So … a plane," Max said. "You're describing, a magic-powered plane?"

"Huh? That is what I described isn't it? OK, that, yes, that's what we need."

"I can make the frame if you can provide the magic."

"I've magic leaking out my ass."

"…right."

Jack spoke up. "I'm no expert in aviation but I can follow instructions. What will you two do?"

"I can think of some things that will keep us occupied." Honey winked at Melissa. "Right, sweet cheeks?"

Melissa frowned at Honey. "Never call me that again."

"No promises!" Honey cut a line in the air with her hand.

"I'll uh, get to work then," Max said, he and Jack leaving to get busy while the other two got busy.

The witches of the jungle had incredibly strict rules about cutting down trees and their makeshift plane ended up being mostly made of reeds tied together with twine. Honey's magic did the bulk of the work in holding it together. She also did some quick fireproofing so Melissa could sit inside without setting the whole thing up in flames.

They made a propeller out of Melissa's feathers, which were, unsurprisingly, as light as feathers but stronger than any earthly substance.

They couldn't manage any glass, so the front window consisted of two layers of a reed mesh screen that wouldn't keep out much air but could avoid the majority of insects.

"What are those things on the bottom?" Honey asked.

"Landing gear, so we can"—Max mimed a plane landing with his hand—"land."

"I figured we'd just crash into the ground."

"Not all of us are invulnerable."

"Right." Honey gave Max a playful punch in the arm. "Good thinking. Geez, you would have died. I always forget how fragile humans are." She clapped her hands together and pulled out a vial of neon purple liquid. "If everything's ready, I'll put the fuel on the propeller."

"You made fuel?"

"Yeah, I thought I'd do something while we waited. Seemed easier than maintaining magic the whole trip. It's supercharged too; it should get us there in no time."

"What's it made out of?"

"Angelic vaginal juice is a major component."

"Honey!" Melissa grabbed the vial out of Honey's hands. "That's what you were doing?!"

"Yes … you seem upset."

"You should have asked first, and also not announced it to everyone. This is embarrassing."

"Wha— I— How? If my vaginal juice could power an airplane I'd tell everyone about it."

"Unbelievable." Melissa slid a hand over her face. "In the future, before you use any of my … fluids, for anything, please ask first, and don't tell anyone about it."

"Alright sorry, I'll ask next time."

"Thank you," Melissa said.

"Can I have the fuel back?"

Melissa handed the vial back over to Honey, who started smearing it on the propeller.

"What is else is in it?" Jack asked.

Honey averted her gaze from Melissa as she worked the fuel into the propellor. "I'd rather not say any more."

"Honey." Melissa moved closer to Honey stretching her wings out behind her. "What else is in it?"

"Nothing! I said I'll ask next time."

Melissa sighed, and moved over to the hatch that made for an entrance. She climbed inside and wrapped her wings around herself in the rear of the plane. Jack sat at what controls there were, which mostly amounted to a stick and another smaller stick. Magic did most of the work. Max poked at the reeds on the walls as if he might make some final adjustment to increase their stability. Honey hurled herself into the plane just as the propeller started.

It did not start in the way plane propellers usually start. A spurt of movement that quickly turns into the blur of the blades. It blazed into life spouting golden flame and purple mist that trailed around the plane as it shot through the sky.

The wind screeched as it moved through the reeds at high speed, the fragile frame shuddering against the magic that held it together. A few sailors would witness the sight as it passed by their ships and most saw it as a bad omen because people who believe in omens usually like them to be bad.

Those on land who saw it breathed a sigh of relief when it passed them by and after managing to make a few days of good gossip out of it, promptly forgot the whole affair. As was the way of things for proper village folk when anything too strange happened.

It would land a few hours after takeoff, near Alteem's house, with Melissa exiting first to stretch her wings and helping Honey out of the hatch with a hand. Max and Jack made for a more unsteady exit. Even after traveling across universes and through space, the wild ride on the magic reed plane did not feel secure. Even knowing the magic would keep it together, it's an altogether different feeling sitting in a bundle of shaking sticks that scream at you as they defy physics.

Honey swept her hand toward the house like a tour guide. "So this is where Alteem lives. I stayed here for a while after I was voluntarily deposed."

"You were what?" Melissa asked.

"Doesn't matter, my daughter came here since I have no idea where Mathew lives. We'll just ask Alteem where she went." Honey knocked on the door of the house, then knocked louder when no one answered. "No one seems to be home; it's OK, I'm just gonna break in."

"Honey, no!" Melissa grabbed on to the witch.

"Oh, it's OK, he's forgiven me for far worse."

"We can just ask people in the nearby town where he is."

"Yeah," Honey said as she eyed the door with an eagerness to break it down. "I suppose that's a practical alternative to property destruction. Not as fun though."

It didn't take much questioning to discover Alteem had left with Alma for Waluigia. They returned to the plane to make the next part of their journey.

"Sooo, we're out of fuel and I did say I'd ask next time." Honey made a lewd gesture with her fingers to Melissa.

"No."

"But, for the plane."

"I said no."

"Alright," Honey said, putting her fingers away. "I can handle a shorter trip easy with just my magic."

"Then why did you ask for my …"

"Because it's hot!"

It took little time to fly to Waluigia in the magic plane, and they could see it on the horizon less than an hour later. "There's a bunch of spaceships above the city," Jack announced.

"What kind, sciencey, alien, criminal, or fascist?" Honey crawled to the wicker window.

"I think fascist."

"Damn, that's the least fun kind. Better land somewhere outside the city."

"I was going to do that anyway. Don't usually land planes inside of cities."

"Maybe you don't."

Jack brought the plane to as smooth a landing as one can expect under the conditions. As they approached the city a group of the metal

81

doll-like soldiers with a woman officer confronted them. "This city is under the protection of the Cosmos Guardians. No one is currently allowed to enter or leave."

Honey squinted at the group. "Do you know who I am?"

"You match the description of the criminal known only as 'the witch.' A resident of this universe and wanted across numerous universes, dimensions, and planes. Her crimes include cannibalism, infanticide, and mass murder to name the worst of them."

"And you think you can stop me?"

"We shall do our duty if it comes to that." The officer put her heels together and stood up straight.

"You know, they don't actually care about you."

"Wha-what?"

"I do know, because I've done the whole authoritarian thing. All the stuff about duty and sacrifice, it's just to get you to do what they need you to do. If you die they'll say you were a hero who died for blah, blah, blah, but the only ones actually crying will be your family."

The officer lost her posture until she snarled and stood stiff again. "You're a criminal of the worst kind who isn't to be trusted."

"Then why don't you arrest me?"

"We have other orders ... for today."

Honey got close to the officer who drew away even if she kept her feet in place. "What other orders?"

"You'll learn when we want you to learn."

"Well then, since you can't be reasoned with." Honey started to walk around the group.

The officer pulled up a tablet and tapped her fingers across it. The metal dolls moved to try to grab the witch, but she snapped her fingers and purple tentacles erupted from the ground to hold them in place before they reached her. Honey stopped and looked at the dolls.

"There are people inside of there." She placed her hand on one of their chests and looked through the faceplate. "What have you done to them?"

"They are the ultimate executors of the law. The sacrifice they made is the greatest honor."

Honey walked to the officer, taking her careful time with each step. "Perhaps I should give you the opportunity to make such a sacrifice."

The officer recoiled, and backed away from the witch.

A smile spread across Honey's face. "Don't quite believe the company line all the way then."

"I … you … we all have a duty."

Honey closed her eyes, and when she opened them again a purple smoke trailed out of their corners. "How eager you are to do your duty, even willing to die for it." She grabbed the officer and held her close. The tendrils of smoke from her eyes started to stroke the officer's face. "There are worse things than death. How much did they tell you about me? Did they tell you of the horrors I can inflict? Death, duty, these things will flee from your thoughts. I can ruin your mind and all that will be left of you is a drooling fool unable to even comprehend what has happened to you. You will forget you were ever anything else. Unable to desire, to think, a husk that was once a person. Any semblance of what could be called a soul seared out of you by things unimaginable."

The officer trembled in Honey's grip, the mist tendril making her whimper, "I … I will not shirk my duty."

Honey released the woman. "Can't blame a girl for trying." Her eyes returned to normal.

"You're not … going to unleash horrors on me?" The officer straightened her uniform and tried to stand up straight again.

"I don't really do that anymore. Shucks right?" Honey kicked the ground. "But I figured I'd try and bluff you. Ya know, to get you to see reason."

"Reason? Why?"

"To help you. Because I've been too far gone, and yet someone reached me. That's why I'm not evil anymore."

"You're not? But, but you still must pay for your past crimes."

"Yup, I'm doing that."

"You need to go to prison."

"Prison?" Honey let out an evil-sounding cackle, which is really the only kind of cackle she knew how to do. "What the hell good would that do? No one can make amends for past wrongs inside a prison. I'm already reformed, so prison can't do that for me."

The officer sputtered a bit before finding her voice again. "Because that's where criminals belong."

"Sorry, but if I go to prison I can't pay the debts I've incurred."

"You—" The officer cut off and touched a hand to her ear. "I read you, sir … but she's right here … yes, sir." The officer addressed Honey again. "We're leaving. I demand you release our soldiers."

Honey shrugged, and waved her hand toward the metal dolls she'd trapped. The tentacles disappeared and the officer pressed some buttons on her pad so the troops followed her.

"Be seeing you soon," she said to the witch.

"The hell does that mean?"

"Come on, Honey." Melissa put an arm over Honey. "Whatever they came here for they're leaving now."

Honey watched as shuttles descended from the ships in the sky to collect the Cosmos Guardians. "They're leaving because they have what they came for. I doubt they came all this way for something insignificant." Honey shrugged again and strode toward the city. "Whatever it is they don't pose a threat to me. If needed I can get it back."

The spaceships phased away, exiting the universe in a flash of red.

CHAPTER 11

The metal dolls herded Mathew and his family into the living room of the house. They'd hidden, but the dolls were made to find people. Nitrel appeared before them, a smug expression on his face, the dolls carrying a bloody Alteem behind him. They threw him down before Alma.

The young witch stared up at him with fury in her eyes. "You should not—"

"Quiet!" Nitrel commanded. He pressed something on his wrist and the metal doll seized Alma, clasping a hand over her mouth. "We studied you for a while, little witchling, and we could not determine what magic you use to bend people to your will. Every sensor we have has come up with nothing, but if you cannot speak, then you cannot influence. We have what we need." He pressed his wrist again and the metal dolls carried Alma away. "She won't be harmed; she's not our target, just bait."

"I won't let you," Alteem said. He lunged for Nitrel, moving with strength and speed despite how badly they'd beaten him.

Nitrel pulled a rod from his side and flicked it. In the same moment a blade erupted from Alteem's chest in a shower of blood.

"So unnecessary." Nitrel moved the rod through the air. Blades and edges of a sword flitted by everyone's vision, like seeing something flicker over the shards of a broken mirror. "This is a multidimensional sword. Quite a handy thing when hunting beings who can move through such things in ways we mere mortals never will. I nearly killed myself several times learning to use it; even I don't know how many dimensions it stretches across. A risk that has paid off more times than I can remember." He put the rod back on his belt and marched away.

Mathew moved to Alteem's side, whose breath strained and bubbled with blood. "Alteem, I'm sorry."

Issa grabbed her medical bag and moved to Alteem's other side. She tried to staunch the bleeding with some nearby bandages, but he was beyond medical help.

"It's alright, Mathew." Alteem coughed, his breath becoming weaker. "I probably should have died a long time ago. Life has given me more than I deserved; I'm glad to go out on one last heroic act. Even if it failed."

Someone knocked on the door.

Mathew did not move for fear he'd miss Alteem's last moments.

"No, this time I'm doing it!" they heard Honey shout before the door shattered into dust. Honey stood in the doorframe, a massive angel behind her, a man in a strange orange and yellow suit, and another in red, white, and black, far more stylish.

"Honey?!" Mathew said. "Alteem is dying."

Marching forward, Honey knelt down next to him.

"Honey." Alteem coughed, blood dripping from his mouth. "I'm glad you're here. I always hoped I might see you one last time."

"You did?" Honey frowned at Alteem, her eyes doubtful.

"Yes, I wanted to tell you I'm proud of you. You raised an amazing daughter."

"Thanks." Honey placed a hand on Alteem's chest.

"Bury me with my people," Alteem said, his eyes slowly closing.

A green and purple swirl appeared in Honey's hand; it filled Alteem's wound and the wound vanished. Alteem's eyes popped open with a gasp.

"You forgot I can heal people, didn't you?"

"I, uh. I was dying; my mind couldn't think clearly."

"So dramatic," Honey said, and got to her feet, looking around. "Where is my daughter?"

Alteem wiped the blood from his mouth. "They took her. Those people from the sky."

Honey's fists clenched; the air darkened. "Those cop sons of bitches took my daughter?" She fell to her knees and tore into the wood on the floor with her hands. The sun darkened until everything went black, except Melissa whose holy glow persisted in the unnatural darkness. "I will invent new agonies to set upon them. Shatter their minds and torture each piece so that they may feel a thousand unique forms of pain at the same time."

"Honey, I know you're upset." Melissa put a hand on Honey's shoulder. "But she'll be OK."

"I know she'll be OK, but they won't be." She took Melissa by the hand and stood up. "Let's go."

Melissa folded Honey's hands in hers. "Slow down. We don't even know where we're going?"

The light slowly returned to the world. "We have a name; we can find them that way."

"OK, but where will we find someone who could even recognize that name? I've never heard of the Cosmos Guardians."

Jack stepped forward. "There's a sort of space station in between universes. Someone there might know something. I could take you to it, at least I could if we had an interuniversal spaceship."

"A what?" Mathew said.

"She destroyed mine," Max said.

"I wouldn't have destroyed your spaceship if you had listened to reason," Honey said.

"I could rebuild it, if I had the right materials, but, uh, things around here aren't exactly on the up and up technologically."

Honey advanced on Max and placed three fingers on his forehead. "I might be able to pull the spaceship from your mind into reality."

"Would it hurt?"

"Yes."

"Would I live?"

Honey glanced to the side. "Yes, forever in our hearts and minds."

"I know we've gotten along better since our first meeting, but we're not at a place that I'm willing to die for you."

Honey dropped her hand. "Alright fine. Maybe if we gather the other heroes they could help build one. They all made it here; some of them must have knowledge about traveling across realities."

"They don't exactly have space-age materials lying around here, much less interuniversal material."

"Metal from hell should be able to do the job," said Honey. "I could call in some old favors, make good on some old threats."

Melissa grabbed Honey's hand. "Are you sure about that? I don't want you going too far. Maybe I should go to hell; I can get what we need. It's easier for me to travel back and forth too."

"Hell's not exactly friendly to angels, Melissa."

"I'm no ordinary angel; I've ventured into many a hell before to rescue those in need."

"Wait," Mathew interrupted. "Melissa?"

"Melicintarifer, but everyone calls me Melissa."

"But"—Mathew motioned to Honey—"you said Melissa was your archnemesis."

Honey shook her head at Melissa. "What? No, I never said that."

"You said, and I quote, 'I hate that bitch.'"

Melissa raised an eyebrow at Honey.

"Don't listen to him; he's an idiot."

"You did say that," Alteem said. "More than once, actually."

"We have more important things to talk about. My daughter's been kidnapped."

Max put a fist on his chin in a thoughtful pose. "I don't fully understand the extent of your magic, but with your powers, my tech expertise and the combined labor of all the heroes we could be able to put together a spaceship capable of traveling across the universe. The real trick would be getting fuel for it. I, uh, I don't know if the same sort of thing would work for the plane."

Honey gave a perverted smile. "I'd have to distill it down to create a more concentrated form, but I could whip up a formula."

"Distill down what?" Issa said. "Maybe I can help."

Honey glanced at Melissa. "I'm not allowed to say."

Melissa, for her part, covered her face with her hand.

Mathew looked back and forth between them. "What? Why not?"

"I don't know why not, Mathew. If my vaginal juice could launch people into space I'd paint that fact on the side of the ship."

"Honey! Please!" Melissa shouted.

"I didn't say anything about your juices, just that if it were my juices I'd be proud."

"OK, I'm going to hell now."

"Don't leave angry."

"I'm not angry." Melissa cupped Honey's face with her hands. "We just need to talk about boundaries when I get back."

"It's not that I want to violate your boundaries; I just think you should be proud of your pussy power."

"I am proud of my"—Melissa took a moment to look at the others and leaned in closer to Honey to whisper—"pussy power; I just don't feel the need to announce it."

"OK good, because you should be. You've got a very valiant vagina."

"You need to stop now."

"OK, but only because vulva also starts with a *v* and I'm struggling to make it work. Can viscous be used as a noun?"

"I love you. I'll be back as soon as I have something useful."

"I love you too, be careful."

Melissa gave Honey a peck on the lips. She then pulled out her molten sword from the air and sliced a rift in reality.

"Wait," Honey said before Melissa could step through. "Luminous labia liquid."

Melissa rolled her eyes, shook her head, and disappeared into the rift.

No one said anything as the rift in reality mended itself.

"There's no way you two were saying what I think you were saying," Issa said, breaking the silence. "You can't possibly intend to power a ship that can travel into space with her …"

"Potent pussy product?"

"Yes … that."

"I'm not supposed to say."

"Right."

Max struck a pose, his hands on his hips and his chest out. "I should be off to locate our wayward would-be avengers. The heroes who came here to slay the witch but were swayed to stay their hands. I do not know the area well."

"I can help you find the way," Alteem said.

Max clasped Alteem on the shoulder. "Let us be off then, friend."

"It can probably wait till the morning."

"So it shall be. I shall sleep under the stars tonight, but first, my pre-sleep workout." Max exited out the back door.

"I'll get to bed then too." Alteem left and went to the guest room.

"I … uh, I'll just find a hotel or something," Jack said, leaving out the front door.

Honey rocked on her heels. "Just the three of us then."

"My husband is the father of your daughter as I understand it," Issa said.

"Yeah, why?" Honey gave a faux punch toward Mathew's wife. "Did you want to even the score?"

"I … no, most certainly not."

"You don't have to be shy, I'm ready and willing. If we're being honest I'm practically always ready and willing. My body count is as high as my body count if you catch my meaning. I'm kidding, obviously; I have no idea what either number is, but I've killed way more people than I've had sex with. Not for lack of trying, but it'll take me millennia to close that gap. I feel like I'm talking to just talk here; what's going on, is this happening? Mathew, are you even breathing right now? Say something, it's freaking me out."

Mathew, for his part, had frozen in place the moment Honey offered to have sex with his wife. Unintentionally he'd achieved the sort of perfect stillness that holy people can meditate for centuries and not accomplish. Though, rather than reaching nirvana, he'd found a plane of personal torment.

"I don't mean to be rude," Issa said, "but I don't think we can. Plus you have your daughter to worry about."

"Honestly, sex relaxes me; it'd help take my mind off things. I don't want to put any pressure on you or anything. Would it change your mind if I told you my breasts are magical?"

"You ... did you use magic to?"

"No, no, not like that. This is all natural, baby." Honey slapped herself on the ass. "I've never used magic to enhance my looks. Although I guess I do use magic to make myself forever young and that's kept everything nice and perky. I guess from a certain point of view you could say I have used magic to enhance my looks, but then look at you, you're close to forty right? Sometimes age only makes things better."

Issa gave a manic, uncomfortable giggle and moved her hand to cover her face before letting it fall. "That's very nice of you to say, but I still don't think—"

"Touch my breasts; see if it changes your mind." Honey thrust her chest toward Issa.

She half reached for Honey's chest, but stopped herself. "I couldn't, we're married and everything."

"We can make it a threesome; I'm down for whatever. I'm just tense with everything going on, you know. Or Mathew could just watch. Whatever works for you guys, honestly, I'm flexible, and I'm flexible; I can get both legs behind my head."

"That's very impressive, but I've never, I couldn't, *we* couldn't." She gestured to Mathew, but he still hadn't moved.

91

"What about my ass?"

"What?"

"Would you like to touch my ass. It's phenomenal. Not as great as Melissa's obviously, but she's an angel; who can compete with that? Still, I'd say it's probably in the top ten thousand asses of all time. I know that's a big number, but I've been to several worlds, hells, heavens, and planes of existence so I've had a very competitive pool."

"I um …" She glanced one more time at the motionless Mathew. "I guess it wouldn't hurt to touch it, just to see."

"Alright then." Honey started to lift up her dress.

"Oh I thought we'd just do it over the clothes."

"If you're gonna touch it, then you should touch it." Honey turned around and backed into Issa.

"OK, why not?" Mathew's wife reached down and gave Honey's tushy a tentative touch. "Wow," she said, digging in a little more. "It's firm, but soft at the same time. Like, the perfect amount."

"Sooo, what do we do then?"

"I've never really … I don't know, Mathew?"

Mathew's eyes, locked straight forward, slowly moved in the direction of the two women.

CHAPTER 12

They'd boarded Alma onto a prison ship. The prisoners were seated in groups of four, chained to their seats with black cords. Lights in the room flickered with every jostle, casting a red glow on all those seated. No windows covered the walls, and the only thing of note besides the prisoners was the metal doll guards that paced up and down between the rows.

The prisoners themselves were mostly human or humanoid. A collection of criminals (criminals according to the Cosmos Guardians anyway) from different universes and both outside and in between. A remarkable thing, that in most cases where the conditions of life naturally occur, you eventually get humans. While opinions differ, the general consensus among scholars of the subject is that this is because most gods are incompetent and not worthy of worship. If they knew what they were doing, obviously we'd get something better, like elves or fairies, maybe even dwarves.

Mixed in among the humans could be seen the occasional creature with strange orifices and skin the shade of a primary color. There were sentient oozes, of course, but their very nature meant transporting them required very specific conditions and so they were not seen here.

One mermaid was among the group, but not nearly so sexy as sailors fantasize. She had skin of all scales, fins on both sides of her head, a dorsal fin instead of hair, and bulbous fishy eyes. Though, if other independent novels are any indication, that's exactly what some of you are looking for. I'd judge you, but I wrote this series and really, I don't know what I was thinking.

Where was I? Alma, being a tiny girl among a nasty crew, looked a bit out of place. Even among other prisoners who might be witches, they tended either toward the hag direction or the leather mommy dom variety. One small girl in what were basically early Renaissance-period clothes, while probably far more similar to anyone historically accused of witchcraft, did not fit in among the varied group of generally bad motherfuckers.

She sat in the third seat of her group of four, on her left a person probably four times her size, several layers of muscle under several layers of fat. The bulges in their body were so big you couldn't even see the black cords strapping them to the chair. Their head was mostly bald except for a pink mohawk three inches long and two inches high. Two beady eyes and bright red lips made up their face with a small tattoo of a rubber duck just under their right eye.

On her right was a scrawny man with a bandage covering the right side of his head. He had a long pointed nose, and one brown eye visible on the uncovered portion of his face. A few bits of stubble poked from his chin. He didn't have a right hand, and both his legs were missing.

The far left seat held a red cube, its sides subtly convex.

"Excuse me," Alma said, as one of the guards walked past them down the aisle, but the guard did not respond.

"They can't hear you," the man on her right said, looking straight forward with a deadness in his eyes. "They can't hear anything anymore."

"Why not?"

"The suit replaces their senses. They are completely cut off from the outside world. Before they go in the suit, they burn out the eyes, poke out their ears—even their nerves are fried. The suit is the only thing that gives them feedback about the world around them. The officers with the pads can turn off the suit sensors at will. Touch them and they don't feel it, but the suit will let them know someone is touching them. Right now the only thing they're aware of is the aisles they need to walk. If anything ends up in the aisles that isn't supposed to be there, then they remove it."

Alma watched the patrolling metal dolls. "Why do that to people? If you want total obedience can't they just use a robot?"

"The Cosmos Guardians don't trust robots. Robots always end up either too stupid or too smart."

She shook her head. "That's not right. They shouldn't do that to people just so they can have total obedience."

The man's eyes shifted in her direction. "Go ahead and tell them that."

"I would, but none of them will talk to me. They use the guards to move me around and whenever I'm in their presence they gag me and put a bag over my head. If they can't hear us, then it should be easy to plan our escape."

The person on her left shivered. "No escape, don't try."

"There's always a way." Alma slid a key card through a small square on her bindings and they came undone. "My name is Alma by the way."

The man on her right turned to look at her. "Where did you get that card?"

Alma held up the key card in one hand; it vanished and appeared in her other hand. "I know a few magic tricks, but I'm best at teleporting small objects. Mostly I practiced with cards so I'm really good at anything card-shaped. For some reason whenever I try to show people they don't want to see it."

"That's impossible. They have magic dampening fields covering the entire ship."

"It doesn't matter if it's impossible; it's magic. The whole point of magic is being able to do the impossible."

"No, there are hard limits to what magic can do, rules that must be followed."

"That's not really magic then is it? You're just describing another natural force. Electricity has hard rules to what it can and cannot do, and it's a natural force, but much of what can be accomplished with it would be viewed as magical to some people. Magic is about breaking rules, defying the limits of reality."

"But then you can just do anything; any problem can be resolved with magic."

"Right, because it's magic. Besides, I already teleported the card so your point is moot."

"I don't really think you teleporting the card is pertinent to the broader philosophical discussion. I just don't think it's narratively satisfying if people can pull any sort of magic out of nowhere to suddenly solve all their problems."

"I get what you're saying, but if magic is completely explainable and has clear rules, then it ceases to be magic. You can call it magic if you want, but it isn't anymore. Magic is mysterious and not completely explainable; that's what makes it magic. The whole point is being able to do things that people shouldn't be able to do."

The man turned forward again. "It doesn't matter, put so much as a hair in the aisle and they'll stun you."

"I'm sure we can come up with something working together. What about you, big fellow, what's your name?"

The big person on her left looked at Alma's removed shackles. "You take off?" they said, and held up their own black cords.

"Of course, we're all in this together after all." Alma removed their shackles.

"Name is Squig," the large person said, stretching out their body in the confined space.

"And you?" Alma used the card on the man to her right's shackles.

"Doesn't matter if you free me, they took away my cybernetic implants. I'm useless now." The person just slid down in their chair as their cords fell away.

"I'm sure that's not true. No one is useless." Alma reached down and touched his arm. "To be is all it takes to have value. Life is its own meaning."

"That's easy for you to say, with your looks, your magic, and your positive attitude. My implants are what made me."

Alma stood back and put her hands on her hips. "Now where is this coming from? Someone put this idea in your head, and I'll tell you they're wrong."

"Say it all you like; it doesn't change anything."

"Right well, you're stubborn, but I hope before our time together is through, you'll learn to value yourself and others."

The man didn't say anything in response.

Alma turned to the cube. "What about you, will you help with the escape?"

Now, it's worth noting that this cube did not speak, exactly. It did communicate in a matter that can best be described as reality warping. It changed reality in small ways to express its point. As it is, not everyone can understand this form of communication. Alma, of course, could, her mother having trained her in all sorts of super-dimensional arts since childhood. I shall of course, as is the way of these things, translate it to English for the sake of convenience. Just for the sake of things, to give you an idea of what communicating with it was like, imagine a vague feeling of unease as you're not quite sure why you feel a certain way but now you suddenly do. Then, "/////////////////<>'^^^^3."

That's basically what it was like.

As to what it actually said. "I am a twelve-dimensional creature. This form you see is merely a piece of my true form, which is beyond your perception. The rest of me is free and elsewhere. Imagine if someone merely placed a cage around one of your fingers and then believed they had captured the whole of you. These fools who call themselves the Cosmos Guardians cannot contain me."

"These fascist cops kidnapped me and are setting up a trap for my mother. If I don't escape and get back to her I'm worried she might do something stupid. Will you please help me?"

The creature gasped, or did what was the equivalent of a gasp for this creature. "Just like Louisa and Parnell when their daughter was kidnapped."

"Exactly."

"Well now I have to help you. I don't want to be like Queen Holly when she refused to lend Louisa her ship."

"Thank you, so much. What's your name?"

Again, it's difficult to express this thing's name, but for the sake of simplicity we'll call it Polly.

"Anyone else?" Alma asked the rest of the room, which, given the volume of the room, most didn't hear. Those nearby grumbled disapproval and one person called her a fool. "There's no need to be a bunch of Grumpy Guses about it. I know if we work together we can all find a way out of here. Also, I have a key card so that should help."

The key card made its way around the room, freeing everyone. Though many still grumbled about the impossibility of the task. "Nothing is impossible with the help of friends," Alma told them.

The man with one arm did not move. "If I had my cybernetic implants, I could hack my way into the ship. From there we could open the doors."

"I'll be your cybernetic implants."

"That doesn't make a lot of sense."

"When we work together, there's nothing we can't do. Polly, any ideas?"

The cube spun in the air and became half a sphere. "I could make a wire that can connect your magic to the electric system, but from there I do not know."

"I rip up floor," Squig said, and they gripped the floor in their hands. The floor crumpled and they pulled up a panel, exposing the ship's wires beneath. An alarm blared, and the lights began to flash on and off in a steady rhythm.

Alma gave Squig a pat on the arm. "Good job, but let's not rush into our actions."

"Sorry," Squig said.

"There's no hope now." The one-armed man continued to slump in his chair.

"Nonsense, we'll just have to work faster. Polly, get me that wire."

Polly spun in the air again; this time a cord appeared around it, like a weed whacker, as it spun. Once it finished Alma took the cord and bent down to the open space in the floor.

"Which wire?" she asked.

The man leaned over enough to look at the collection of wires. "The mustard yellow one."

"Squig, if you would, but be careful not to hurt yourself."

Squig reached down and yanked the yellow cord out. The electricity sparking off the edge of it. Alma attached the cord to the exposed end and then wrapped the rest around her hand. "Woo, that tingles." She reached her hand toward the one-armed man.

"This won't work," he said. "There are magic dampening fields."

"It's magic; it can do the impossible."

He took her hand, and they both gasped. "I … I can see it," he said. "There are a bunch of unicorns and rainbows, but I see the cyber interface."

"The unicorns and rainbows are probably because it's being filtered through me."

"Yeah, of course,"

"Can you get the door open?"

"First I'm slowing down the officers headed our way. That'll buy us a little more time. Now give me a moment." The doors slid open with a very sci-fi sounding *shunk*. "Any ideas for getting past the guards?"

Alma detached the cord from the wire. "One just came to me. The guards are all connected, right? That's how they can all receive orders at once."

"That's right."

She reached for one of the guards as it passed, wrapping her cord around it.

"The hell are you doing?" The man reached to stop her.

The guard stopped, and turned to Alma. It lifted its hand, the palm opening up to reveal a hole that started to glow red. Alma reached forward and pressed her hand against the guard's hand, wrapping her fingers around it.

"They can't feel you," the man said, surprise in his voice that the guard had not already blown off her hand.

"But they still know someone is holding their hand, even if they can't feel it. Whatever else they have done to them, they cannot take away their humanity. Go now all of you. Squig, carry the man who won't tell anyone his name."

Squig nodded, and picked up the man.

"Wait, what about you?" the man called back as Squig carried him away.

Alma turned and smiled as the prisoners crowded their way out the doors. "Don't worry, I'll follow once everyone's out."

The group of prisoners made their way out of the prison ship. They'd expected some resistance from the metal doll guards, but Alma held them all in her grasp. She still held the hand of one of them in the room they'd put all the prisoners in. None of the prisoners understood it, but most assumed she performed magic.

She did not. The metal dolls could no longer feel, at least, not through their normal senses. Alma knew better; even if their nerves were gone the sensors in their suits still told them if something touched them, and since all metal dolls were in constant communication, holding the hand of one was holding the hand of them. Not a single one of them had known such a gesture since they'd been placed inside their new skin. Everyone else saw what the Cosmos Guardians wanted them to see. Dead machines devoid of feeling, but people still lived inside the shells. Even they'd forgotten this; with a simple gesture, they remembered.

The rest of the prisoners escaped on shuttles as the officers scrambled trying to figure out why their perfect soldiers were no longer obeying orders. Not until one of the officers got the courage to investigate the situation themselves, did they find Alma and the metal doll holding hands.

The officer had black hair and pale skin, dressed in the same uniform as the rest of them. He ran forward and knocked Alma's hand away. The metal doll turned, its hand opening up to reveal a hole that started to glow red. The officer pulled up his pad and pressed a button on it that caused the doll to drop its hand.

"What did you do to them, witch?" the officer asked.

Alma stood up straight, indignant. "What did *you* do to them?"

The officer pulled back. "We, they made the ultimate sacrifice for their duty."

"What convenient lies people tell themselves so that they may ignore atrocities. I never will."

"It's not, no," the officer said. "They're volunteers."

"Even so, is this really necessary? Or is it just what makes things easier for those in charge? If they're already willing to fight, then why?"

"I don't know, maybe you're—"

A voice came in from the officer's pad. "Officer Crensly! Do not engage in conversation with the prisoner! Exit the room now."

Crensly shook his head. "Stay away from me, witch!" He pushed her away and ran out of the room. The metal dolls followed out of the room, and the doors were closed, leaving Alma alone.

CHAPTER 13

Honey sat reclined in a chair at the kitchen table, her leg draped over another chair. The heel of her foot gently tapped the back of the chair as it swayed. A breakfast of scrambled eggs and toast lay on the table before them. "You two seem tense; did you not have a good time? I know I did."

Issa and Mathew both sat on the other side of the table, their hair a mess, cups of coffee in their hands. Mathew did not say anything, but took a sip from his coffee.

"We uh, yes, yes I enjoyed myself. Never thought I'd ever do anything like that." She too, took a sip from her coffee.

"You came right? I've been trying to improve. I know you came, Mathew, that's why I'm having a light breakfast, eh? But, Issa, be honest, I want the feedback."

Mathew took a bigger drink from his coffee, even though it scalded his mouth.

"Yes, twice actually."

"Nice! High five." Honey raised her hand.

"What's a high five?"

"Right." Honey lowered her hand. "This fucking planet sometimes."

A golden rift opened in the air and Melissa stepped through.

Honey hopped to her feet and embraced Melissa with a leaping hug. "Sweetie, you're back. I was so worried."

Melissa let Honey back down to the floor and stroked her head. "Everything went fine. I secured a deal for a large quantity of hell metal, but they want you to remove someone named Trexavar from a place called the Soul Tempest. They said you're the only one who could ever do it."

"Classic Trevor," Honey said with a shake of her head. "I can hop down there and pull him out no trouble. He'll probably just be stuck again in a century or so."

"What did you get up to here?"

"We had a threesome."

Mathew let out a series of sputters as he choked on his coffee.

"How did it go?"

"Great, I made Issa cum twice." Honey held up her fingers to indicate the number.

"Good for you." Melissa ruffled Honey's hair. "I told you you were getting better."

"I know, but I'm the only person you've ever had sex with. It's nice to get some confirmation from someone with more experience."

Issa cleared her throat. "I haven't had that much experience."

"Yeah right." Honey strolled back to the table. "No one suddenly puts a pinky up your ass unless they've been around the block at least a couple of times?"

"That's … no." Issa hid her face behind her coffee cup.

Honey grabbed a piece of toast from the table. "You mortals get so weird about this stuff. I'll be back in a few weeks; try not to have too much fun without me." She blew the couple a kiss. This only made them shrink down in their chairs.

Melissa and Honey disappeared through the golden rift, which closed behind them. Max and Alteem came through the back door not long after. Alteem sat at the table, but Max grabbed a piece of toast and started doing squat thrusts while eating the toast.

"So." Alteem dished himself up some food and dug in. "Sleep well?"

"Yes," Mathew said without so much as a pause. "And that's all we did."

Alteem gave him a look, but let it go. "Where's Honey?"

"She went with Melissa to finish securing the hell metal." Issa put her coffee down and put some eggs on her plate. "Said she won't be back for a few weeks."

"Just as fine; from what Jack said it'll probably take us as much time to find the heroes and bring them back here."

They finished breakfast with little more conversation, and Alteem and Max departed.

Max didn't know the land terribly well, but with Alteem's help they found their way back to the group of heroes. At this point they'd begun constructing a makeshift village, and given the disparate technology level, one of wildly different architectural styles. The tools available were still limited so it's not like anyone had automatic doors or anything.

Max gathered everybody up. "OK, so, obviously the plan to get people home by the solstice had a bit of a hiccup. Long story short, we had a short trip to heaven, got stuck on the other side of the world, and flew in a magic plane back here. Any questions?"

Most of the people there raised their hands.

"Oh boy," Max said. He did a quick stretch of his arms to ready himself. "Alright, let's do this. We'll start with you, the muscular woman dressed in leopard skins."

"What is heaven?" the woman asked in a gravelly voice.

"Ah right, so, does your culture believe in an afterlife or some sort of underworld for the dead?"

The woman nodded.

"Right, so, it's like that. Heaven is a place where the creator of this universe lives, or I should say lived, and he brought up people to worship him forever. OK, um, you, the young gentleman with a red tunic and tiara."

"What's a plane?"

"OK, yeah, I should've guessed not all of you would know what that is. It's a flying machine." Several hands went down after that. "You, the guy with an impractically large sword."

"What do you mean the other side of the planet?"

"I ... I thought we went over this. The planet is round."

"No, no, the planet is a bowl supported by a tower of insects who burrow slowly up from the earth."

An eruption of groans occurred in the crowd. "Ug'grug, we've explained this to you a million times," someone said.

"No, no, I don't believe this science nonsense. I can see with my eyes that the earth is bowl-shaped, and where do all the insects come from if there isn't an infinite tower of them beneath the ground? It's the only thing that makes sense."

Jack shook his head. "I assume we're all willing to move past this." Everyone but Ug'grug nodded. "Right, we've a new plan for getting everyone home. We're building a spaceship—" Several hands went up. "It's like a ship that can travel through the air. It'll be able to cross universes. We need it to rescue Honey's daughter, who's been kidnapped by fascist cops, but we can also use it to get everyone home. That said, building it will be quite the effort so we're going to need to work together. Those from technologically advanced civilizations will obviously be a boon, but even anyone being able to haul things will be useful. Everyone got that?" People mostly mumbled assent.

"I don't see why we should help her rescue her daughter," said one redheaded woman with a bow and dressed in black skintight leather clothes.

"How are you even able to move in that outfit?" Max asked.

The woman looked at her own outfit as if it was occurring to her for the first time how impractical it was. "I ... I don't know."

Alteem stepped forward. "The answer is because you're all heroes, and a good person is in trouble. You came here hoping to accomplish something good, but revenge doesn't right wrongs; it just makes more of them. I learned from someone wiser than myself that swords don't make a hero; helping people does."

"What about guns?" someone shouted.

"Or robot mechs?" someone else said.

"I'm not clear on what those are, but probably not. A good person has been taken by bad people; as heroes you couldn't ask for a more black-and-white situation than that. Don't you want to go back home and tell people you accomplished something while you were here?"

"I'm the last of my kind."

"Yeah, me too."

"Also me."

A few more people spoke up.

Max raised his hand. "I'm also, the last of my kind, since everyone else is chiming in."

"Honestly, you're probably not. I thought I was, but Honey has proven to be quite bad at genocide. There are quite a number of people on this planet who thought they were the last but they weren't. When you get back, search around a bit; I promise you'll find someone. She had a real lack of work ethic during her genocidal maniac era."

This news left quite a few of the last of their kinds excited.

Alteem gestured across the crowd. "Everyone ready to save what I promise is the best person you'll ever meet?"

He'd been hoping for a hurrah but mostly got mild assents and nods. "It'll do," he grumbled to himself and everyone gathered their belongings to prepare for the journey.

Hell, or at least, this particular hell, as we established in the first novel, is hot and humid to an agonizing degree. You might hear the occasional scream of the tortured damned depending on your location, but you're far more likely to have a demon walk up to you and ask, "Hot enough for you?" then laugh at what they just said, no matter how many times they've said it before.

Honey hopped up and down and pointed to a pot of boiling black ooze where people kept trying to climb out only to slide back in once they reached the edge, howling in agony the entire time. "Right over there, that's where I had my first orgy. Honestly it was terrible; took forever to clean all that ooze off of me. You think getting cum out of your hair is hard? Try black tar."

Melissa did her best to respond with enthusiastic support, but she'd not been made to lie. "That's uh … that's awful, Honey. I have no idea how you could look back fondly at that."

"Just nostalgic I guess; hell always gets me that way." Honey sighed as they continued their journey to the Soul Tempest. "I was so young then, never could keep up with all the sex demons. I tried, but those people know how to take fucking to a new level, and since it's hell that level is a basement level. Sex with angels is way better—counterintuitive I know—but the heavenly sexual repressions make you a kinky lot, but not sex demon kinky. I can't count how many times they tried to talk me into letting them brand me. Why would I do that to my skin?"

"Maybe let's not talk about sex demons."

Honey looped her arm around Melissa's. "Sorry, I didn't mean to make you uncomfortable. The boiling ooze pit just brought back some memories. This is way before I met you; I wasn't even a hundred years old. You never talk about your past."

"I have no past. First came the war, and after that I had nothing. I didn't mind; I believed I'd done my duty and after that I merely existed. My life truly began when I met you. I believed happiness was something I'd given to others but not meant for me."

"I'd hardly say I made you happy."

"You did when you weren't off causing chaos. I never hated you, but you insisted on making choices that weren't good for you and really weren't good for other people. All those days I kept hoping you'd choose me instead of running off to do something else. It's not fair of me, but I can't help feeling hurt that someone else could do for you something I never could."

"I'm sorry, I just couldn't accept that someone like you could ever actually love someone like me. Not for nothing, but I might be the hottest messiest hot mess to ever be a hot mess. Even now I feel like if you knew everything I did you wouldn't be able to handle it."

"I never cared about what you'd done, even now. Claire forged me out of pure goodness. Forgiveness comes pretty naturally to me. It's only what you continued to do that I didn't know how to save you from. Like I wasn't good enough."

"You're amazing; if anything you were too good. I didn't think I deserved you and so I drove you away on purpose. Only after I got everything I thought I wanted did I realize that I might even be capable of making the choices I needed to. You didn't fail me; the timing just didn't work. Every time we got together I always knew you'd leave so I made sure of it. Now I realize, you always came back. Thank you, for never giving up on me completely."

"As if I could ever stay away from that smile. That chaotic, mad smile."

They came to a swirling tempest of blue and black. A chorus of screams rushed by them as souls caught in the tempest were whipped around. In the center of the tempest the winds tore at the souls, taking pieces of them off until nothing remained and they became part of the winds. The process took millennia and next to the tempest Honey and Melissa appeared little more than ants next to a tree.

Honey let out a low whistle. "He must have been stuck here for a couple of decades for the tempest to get this big."

"So the size is not normal?"

"No, the winds are supposed to filter out through the bottom where they become souls again; then they're pulled back around to the top where they get torn apart all ad infinitum."

"Maybe I shouldn't interfere with hell, but I want to stop this."

"Alma, my daughter, helped start a demon reform school. So far, it hasn't gone super well, but it's a start. Eventually the hope is they can turn hell into a nice place, but for now, we can't do anything about this without massive repercussions back in the mortal plane."

"Didn't killing God have some repercussions?"

"Weirdly, it didn't seem to. I don't think he did much of anything anymore. I guess no one else got into heaven, but as you saw, we probably did those people a favor."

"Where's this Trevor?"

"Mmm, kind of everywhere. Right, here we go." Honey stretched her arms behind her back and stepped into the tempest. The winds buffeted her, but her magic reflected it away in flashes of light. A purple miasma oozed off of her and the wind whisked it away in long trails. It grew as the wind continued to carry it, a long trail that started to consume the wind as it carried through the tempest.

Honey's eyes tinted purple, growing brighter until they glowed. Then the light began to pour out of her mouth and fingertips. Spreading from there until it consumed her—a spot of neon purple moving to the center of the tempest, blazing brighter and brighter.

Once the miasma consumed the tempest, purple hands reached out of the winds and gripped the ground, digging it up as the winds pulled at them. The wind slowed, and grew to a stop as the magic hands increased in number to hold it in place.

The blazing spot of neon purple approached the middle of the tempest, where tendrils just as bright burst and snapped to different parts of the tempest like lightning. They contracted, stretching and pulling something from the winds and the ground. A bloody black ooze that dripped and flopped as the tentacles siphoned it from the air.

The process of pulling the ooze out of the tempest took longer than it'd taken to conquer the tempest. The ooze pulsed and pulled against the tentacles, sometimes slipping through their grasp before being grabbed again. As they drew closer to the center the black substance merged together, which only made it harder to drag.

Eventually the tentacles managed to bring all the masses together, and they coalesced into a mass of limbs and faces. New limbs would emerge from the faces, sometimes clawing their way out of the mouth, other times popping out of the eyes. As they did so the faces would split apart into bloody messes until the flesh fell off the body. Faces would also emerge from the limbs, chewing their way out of them or just bursting out in a sprawl of blood, splitting the limbs apart. The limbs too would fall off the body once the faces completed their emergence.

Sometimes the main body became more faces than limbs, but then the balance would shift the other way.

The flesh left behind quickly decayed, maggots appearing in an unnaturally fast life cycle. The flies that emerged from these maggots quickly formed a swarm that followed the main body around. They died fast, creating a rain of flies. The stench of death filled the air, putrid and strong.

"Hon-ey?" the body said, though its words were broken and sounded different since different mouths spoke each syllable before a limb started to emerge. "Is, that, you?"

"Hey, Trevor. Let's get out of here."

"O-K," the demon said as Honey led it back to Melissa.

Honey's blazing purple dimmed quicky, but the hands held the tempest in place until the two forms exited from its edge. Once outside, Honey let the magic go and the tempest began to churn to life again, though its size diminished to that of a natural tornado.

"Ahhh-hhh!" Trevor screamed as they got close to Melissa. "It's, an, an-gel!"

"It's fine." Honey reached to put a comforting hand on Trevor, but the limb she reached for fell off so she just pulled away. "She's my girlfriend, Melissa."

Melissa gave a wave.

"Me-lis-sa? But, you, said, she, was, your, arch-ne-me-sis."

"No, I don't think I said that."

"You, said, and, I, quote, 'I, hate, that, bitch.'"

"This isn't about me right now, Trevor. How come you keep getting stuck in the Soul Tempest?"

"It's, the, on-ly, way, for, me, to, get, souls. All, the, se-xy, de-mons, can, get, souls, easy, but, no, one, wants, to, sell, their, soul, to, this." Trevor might have gestured toward themself, but it wasn't clear.

"Uh"—Melissa raised her hand—"does … does it hurt to be you?"

Trevor's body shifted. "No, not, ex-act-ly. I, might, com-pare, it, to, some-thing, but, it's, the, on-ly, way, I've, ev-er, been."

Honey created a magic umbrella to stop the flies raining on her. "Why do demons want souls anyway?"

"Uh, I, don't, know. Brag-ing, rights, I, think."

"This is the problem with hell; you're always competing. If demons could just learn to cooperate with each other hell would be a much better place."

"That's, not, very, de-mon-ic."

"You're demons, everything you do is demonic. Maybe it's time to change the script on what being a demon really means. Where better for change to begin than a demon whose form is constantly changing?"

"I, don't, know; they'd, just, make, fun, of, me, if, I, tried, to, be, nice."

"Who cares what they think?" Melissa said. "It's not about them; it's about you. Do you want to spend your time chasing after souls until you get caught in some hellish trap, or do you want to be the best version of yourself?"

"I'm, not, sure; I've, ne-ver, tried, to, be, bet-ter." Trevor's body flopped to the side.

"I think it's time to start looking inward, Trevor," Honey said. "You demons need to start asking yourselves the tough questions. Don't use being a demon to excuse your behavior; instead take responsibility for Trevor being Trevor."

"I, guess, I've, got, some, think-ing, to, do."

"We believe in you, Trevor," Melissa said. One of Trevor's faces smiled before a leg erupted from its mouth, and then it flopped away, sometimes managing to stand briefly before the legs burst open with a face and fell off.

The two departed from Trevor, making their way to a place where a portal could be opened from out of hell.

"I ... this isn't coming from a place of judgment," Melissa said. "But I need to ask. Have you had sex with that?"

Honey laughed, tossing her umbrella aside. "No, no, of course not. We tried once, but it's just not physically possible."

CHAPTER 14

The construction of the frame of the spaceship went quicker than expected. It didn't hurt having an all-powerful witch for the shaping and welding of the hell metal.

After the ship finished, Max brought Honey to the spaceship one morning, and gestured broadly to its form. "It turned into that overnight."

The spaceship had a similar form to the one Max first arrived in. The cylinder thicker on the back and tapering to a point on the front. A series of engines on its rear and three fins on the back half. The hell metal was a dull red; spikes had sprouted out of the ship in threatening arrays. Screaming faces appeared in other places, frozen in expression as they jutted from the metal. A series of skulls surrounded the center of the ship.

"Yeah," Honey said. "Hell metal will do that."

Max looked over the ship. "It doesn't exactly look, heroic."

Honey shrugged. "Appearances can be deceiving. Look at me; you'd never guess I'd had a child."

"Yes, you do seem too young for an adult child."

"No, I meant because my body doesn't show any signs. Look how perky my tits are!" Honey thrust her tits in Max's direction.

"I don't think I want to—"

"I said look!"

Melissa flew next to them. "Honey, stop trying to make Max look at your tits."

"But they're so perky."

"I know, they're my favorite, but Max doesn't want to."

"Fine, his loss." Honey unthrust her tits. "I don't want to be rude or anything, but how come you're not into my boobs? Even gay men appreciate a nice pair."

"I don't know," Max said, grabbing a welding torch to cut off some of the spikes. "I'm just not. Even as a teenager I never understood why everyone else was so obsessed with sex."

"My mom used to have to spray me with a water bottle to stop me humping the furniture. Puberty was rough."

Melissa put her arm around Honey. "Puberty is rough for everyone."

"You didn't even have a puberty."

"People tell me things."

"I had to fantasize about the scarecrow coming to life to fuck me because there was no one else around. I still get a little turned on whenever I see one."

Melissa said nothing.

Max gave up on cutting off the spikes after the third one regrew. "You didn't ever try to have sex with the scarecrow did you?"

"We all do stupid things as teenagers, and what I may or may not have done with a wooden penis that I whittled is none of your business."

Melissa and Max averted their gaze.

"Ugh, you two have to be so fucking perfect; you've never committed genocide, not even by accident."

Melissa raised a hand. "You've committed genocide by accident?"

"Oh shit." Honey slapped her forehead. "Pen 5, Max, I remember now. That wasn't my fault; I mean, directly at least."

"What?" Max dropped his welding torch.

"That scientist, Dr. What How's Key. He tricked me."

"Dr. Whachosky?"

"Yes. He told me he was going to cure some disease or something, but really he unleashed a terrible zombie plague on his people."

"That's impossible." Jack sat on the ground. "He … he united us in our fight against the zombies."

"Exactly!" Honey pounded her fist in her hand. "He had a plan to unleash the zombies and then save everyone from the zombies so he could take over. Guess phase two of the plan didn't go so well."

"Why did you help him?" Melissa asked.

"He complimented my hair." Honey twirled a finger through her hair. "And I'd just had the accident so I felt really insecure at the time."

"I built a statue to that man." Jack pounded his fist on the ground once, then repeatedly. "That son of a bitch killed us all!"

"I'm super sorry; I don't know what to do about this."

"Can you bring people back from the dead?"

"I can, but—"

"They don't come back the same, yeah, yeah, but is it still them? If you brought Dr. Whachosky back to life and I killed him, would it be him I'm killing or just a demon in his place or something?"

"There's an interesting philosophical quandary I didn't expect." Honey tapped a finger on her chin. "I do have to anchor the soul to the body, but it's not in control."

"But it would hurt him right."

"Absolutely."

"And it can be done repeatedly?"

"Oh yeah, as many times as you like."

"Then after we take everyone else home, we're going to my home."

"It's a date, and maybe since your home planet isn't habitable anymore you'll let me blow it up."

"What?"

"We'll discuss it later."

Melissa tugged on Honey's sleeve. "Honey, could I talk to you in private for a second?"

Honey wiggled her eyebrows. "Right away, baby."

"Not for sex."

"But we need the fuel! We have an excuse to do it as much as we want."

"Just come over here." Melissa pulled Honey to the side. "I don't know if repeatedly murdering his former hero would be the most healthy thing for Max."

Honey looked over at Max. "You don't?"

"No, he's in pain right now. He just found out a person he thought tried to save his people is the reason they all died. Instead of indulging him, you should comfort him."

Honey crossed her arms. "But I'm already trying to help him."

"Sometimes what people want, isn't what they need. Like how you thought you wanted to conquer the world, but you actually wanted love and acceptance."

"I'm bad at comforting people; you go comfort him."

"If I touch him he'll burst into flames and turn to ash."

"How many times are you going to use that excuse?"

"Every time it applies."

"Fine." Honey stomped her feet. "I'll try."

Honey walked back over to Jack, shooting a couple of looks over her shoulder at Melissa. She sat down next to him. "Melissa thinks, maybe it's not the best idea to repeatedly murder the same person over and over again through the use of necromancy."

"He's the man who made me want to be a hero."

"Alright, well, it's like you told me. When something terrible happens you can use it as an excuse to do terrible things or as an excuse never to do terrible things."

"That was a quote from him."

"Fuck, really? I guess just because you're a shitty person doesn't mean you can't come up with some great advice. I'm trying to help, but I'm out of my depth; I don't know how to comfort people."

"You had a daughter; how did you comfort her?"

"I just held her until she felt better."

"OK."

"Really?"

"Maybe I'm supposed to be tough right now, or a stoic hero, but everything I based my life around is a lie. Someone just holding me is exactly what I need."

"Sure, I'll do that." Honey put her arms around Jack and he let his head drop against hers. "It's possible I've been overthinking this in the past. I think it goes without saying stuff like this is why I never relied on an undead army. They're just not worth the effort. Plus, the smell, woof. Doesn't matter how hot I am if I smell like death all the time. You can't have sex with the zombies. OK, yeah, sure, you can, but a person has to draw the line somewhere. I'm a shameless slut, but I ain't hopping on a dead guy's dick. Girl's gotta have standards … vampires don't count obviously. They're dead, but they're not rotting. It's not as great as the literature makes it seem anyway. You get that moment someone touches the vampire and goes 'You're so cold,' but somehow that doesn't come up during the sex part. Have you ever had someone touch you when they've been outside on a chilly day? Imagine it's the person's whole body and they're thrusting into you. Doesn't matter how hot they look; there's just no way to make that enjoyable. And as far as vampire pussy goes, just get ice cream. It tastes better, doesn't want to bite you, and is roughly the same temperature. Also—"

"Please stop talking."

"Sorry."

CHAPTER 15

The day of departure arrived and the small horde of heroes assembled outside the spaceship. Those qualified received positions, while the rest were assigned under them to learn about spaceship operation.

A brown-haired boy with a blue sword approached Honey. "Some of us, have some concern about the spaceship."

"What about it?"

"It looks kind of evil."

Honey examined the spaceship. "How so?"

"The spikes and the skulls mostly."

"That's just the hell metal. It does that."

"Being made of hell metal doesn't make us feel any better."

"What if we gave it a friendly paint job?"

The brown-haired boy looked at the heroes behind him who shrugged and nodded. "That might help. Do we have time to paint it?"

"I have a spell for painting things."

"You do?"

"I have my reasons. We haven't come up with a name; maybe everyone should discuss it."

This discussion turned out to be a mistake, as the debate would last several hours and get extremely heated. I don't see much point in covering the whole debate here as it's not very interesting in and of itself. The highlight is that people broke into several small factions that each preferred their own name. These factions started to compromise and join together in the hopes of outnumbering the others, which only encouraged more joining and compromising. The end result being two factions mostly split between the heroes and the antiheroes. After two hours, Honey insisted they needed to reach a final compromise and thusly the ship was christened the *RainbowDeath*.

Honey gave the ship a baby blue and soft yellow striped paint job, with red on the fins. The name of the ship on the side involved the letters in "Rainbow" each being a different color and the "Death" portion being metallic letters with an adorable tiger kitten above them looking like one of its paws clawed into the letters.

With everyone boarded and final preparations seen to, Mathew and Issa came to Honey.

"Honey," Mathew said. "Can we talk to you?"

"Sure, but I'm telling you now I don't have time for a farewell threesome. You should have asked during the debate. We'd be able to all sorts of freaky stuff in that time frame."

"No, that's not … Alma is my daughter too, and after discussing it we decided we want to come with you."

"What about your other kids?"

"Their grandparents agreed to take care of them," Issa said.

"Aren't their grandparents dead?"

"Not on my side of the family."

"People get two sets of grandparents?! Actually that makes sense now that I think about it. I just never questioned what my mother told me before now. Alma's grandparents were both dead so it never came up. Holy crap, my grandparents could be alive! No, no, they'd be way too old. What if they had other kids? OK, that's why my mother lied about it, so I wouldn't meet any of my cousins. Sorry, this is all hitting me. Yes you can come with. I need to go somewhere and sit the fuck down."

Honey boarded the spaceship from the stairs that lowered on its side with Mathew and Issa behind her. She pointed the couple in the direction of the ship lodgings coordinator and went to the room she shared with Melissa.

They had the largest room on board, out of necessity not privilege. The ship being made of hell metal did stop Melissa from damaging it with her wings, but they still needed to fit somewhere.

"Something the matter?" Melissa asked when Honey entered the room. She'd been sitting alone staring at the wall. While concerning behavior for a human, it wasn't unusual for an angel who lacked the biological capacity for boredom.

"I might have living family. I think they'd be my seventieth cousin removed or so, but I didn't think even that was possible. Hit me harder than I expected. I think it's also being reminded my mom lied to me about so many things. I'm not really past her."

"I know, come here." Honey nestled into Melissa, which wasn't easy with Melissa's armor.

"I hope you don't just sit in the room the whole trip."

"I wanted to use the pool, but since I'd make the water boil I'll have to wait until the swing shift."

"There's a pool?"

"Yeah, and a hot tub, but every body of water is a hot tub for me."

"We have to have sex in it. Oh, no, we can't; we need to save all of your super snatch snail slime."

"No, Honey, no, never call it that again."

"Yeah, you're right, I went too far that time. I just wish there were a way to find out if I have living family."

"There is the cosmonautical DNA database."

Honey's head snapped in Melissa's direction. "The what?"

"Wait, I know of a place you've never heard of."

"OK, yeah, but what is it?"

"This has never happened before." Melissa got to her feet and started pacing about the room. "You've been to so many more places than I have. Plus I've spent a lot of time chasing after you."

"I'm glad you love this, but I've spent the past few decades on this world, so let's not get too cocky here."

"It might never happen again since we're together now. I need to milk this for all it's worth."

"Just tell me, please?"

"It's hot when you beg."

"OK, I'm excited you're having all sorts of sexual awakenings these days, but tell me, I'll do anything."

"No, I think first you'll do anything, then I'll tell you."

The ship took off into space, overseen by Max and piloted by Jack. For those who hadn't known about space before hunting down Honey, the trip exposed them to new wonder and terror. The first minute or so being the most intense experience of their lives, and considering some of these people had slain dragons that's saying something.

Once in space, routine took over the ship. They made the jump to hyperspace so Jack could take them to a weak point in the universe. From there they'd travel into the greater cosmos.

For Alteem's part, he'd been appointed a moral officer. He spent most of his time getting to know the other heroes. Listening to their stories and figuring out the best ways to keep everyone occupied on board.

Taking a break, he found the mess hall mostly empty and decided to enjoy a little downtime with some tea. That's when Honey burst in, out of breath, her hair a mess, and covered in sweat.

"Everything all right?" he asked as she stumbled over to one of the sinks, grabbed a cup and filled it up.

"I've created a monster," she said before chugging the glass of water, some of it spilling down the sides of her face.

"What, where? Could it damage the ship? Do we need to—"

"No, not literally."

"Oh, don't scare me like that."

"I meant my girlfriend. I've been encouraging her to explore more sexually; she's gone from wilting flower to demanding dom much faster than anticipated. Don't get me wrong, I'll take any role happily, but I'm only human here."

"I don't need to hear about this."

"Sorry, I'm just here to rehydrate and get some carbs. She said she's not done with me yet." Honey filled up her glass again before downing it. "She's so hot, right?"

"Not my type, honestly."

Honey had been in the middle of her third glass of water, but she turned to Alteem, water dripping out of her mouth as she spoke. "The fuck did you just say?"

"Sorry, I just don't really see it."

Honey advanced on Alteem, the top of her dress wet from the water she'd spilled. "Have you lost your mind? I've been through heavens and hells, hundreds of universes, places that the mortal mind isn't capable of comprehending, and that angel is the hottest creature in all of existence."

"I don't know what to tell you. I think she's OK, but I wouldn't call her the most attractive. Why are you so upset? You like her; isn't that enough?"

"If I told you I preferred shit to champagne you'd think I'd gone crazy too."

"I don't know what champagne is."

"It's a sparkling white wine."

"Then I don't know why you'd use an alcohol metaphor when neither of us drinks."

"Fair point." Honey stuffed a piece of bread in her mouth and spoke over it. "But she's prefect. What about her do you not find attractive?"

"I'm afraid if I say you'll only get madder."

"I'm not mad; I'm concerned there might be something wrong with you, OK?"

"First off. She doesn't have real eyes. Just those glowing golden orbs. You can't even tell where she's looking. I like to be able to look into the eyes of someone I love. The golden skin doesn't do anything for me either. I'm not crazy about the wings, and honestly, her butt's too big for me."

"How dare you?"

"See, this is what I was saying."

"Her ass is the greatest ass that has ever been and ever will be. It was sculpted by a god to win the ultimate war against evil and it did. Hundreds of epic poems have been written about it."

"Were they all written by you?"

Honey grabbed a bagel and started eating it plain. "I don't see how that matters."

"I don't wanna upset you, but I'm just being honest here."

As Honey ate her food she continued to rant, crumbs spitting out as she did so. "Believe me when I say that you will never know the heavenly glory that is having sex with that creature. One, because you can't touch her without burning to ash, and two, because she says she needs to have an emotional connection with someone in order to have sex with them. Seriously, can you believe that? The only two people she's ever had an emotional connection with are me and her god. I tried to get something going there, but she said it felt too close to incest, so I didn't push it."

"I'm not really sure what point you're trying to make with all this."

"Yeah, I lost the thread on that one. My broader point is she's awesome, and you'd be lucky to even see her ass, but she said she'd only let someone watch if it was my birthday and I don't remember when that is anymore. So there."

"Not everybody is into the same thing. You're just going to have to learn to live with that."

"I am not." Honey grabbed a tower of sandwiches off a display and started edging toward the door. "This conversation is not over, but I need to get back soon or else I'll be punished. As much as I'd be into that, I promised to be a good girl and I intend to keep that promise." Honey put another sandwich in her mouth before scooping up an armful of food and drinks. She backed out of the room glaring at Alteem before dashing down the hall, the sandwich falling out of her mouth as she did so.

Alteem returned to his tea.

124

Chapter 16

Alma remained alone in a prison cell. No one spoke to her, no one got close to her, and they delivered her food via drone. Her circular cell sat in the middle of a room, which itself made a circle, ten feet from the bars of her cell to the walls of the room, including the domed ceiling. Cameras watched the cell at all times, which was definitely pervy, but what do you expect from the police? She did, in time, figure out which angles the cameras couldn't see her from.

Since they never sent anyone into the room, the only thing that came into her cell was the drone delivering her food. With her ability to teleport small objects from one place to another, Alma began to steal pieces from the drones. Bit by bit, day by day, she managed to amass parts and built a device outside the view of the cameras.

So far, she hadn't aroused any suspicion. Which isn't exactly true. One of the engineers in charge of the maintenance of the drones noticed something wrong. Since each drone only sent food to the prisoners, he deduced one of the prisoners must be responsible for the slow accumulation of missing parts. He couldn't figure out how, exactly, but the conclusion remained a logical one. What this engineer failed to realize is that logical conclusions have no place in police organizations, especially fascist ones like the Cosmos Guardians.

After he submitted his report, his superiors figured he must be guilty since their perfect prison system would never allow prisoners to steal parts unnoticed.

Meanwhile, Alma built her device and presently used it to put markings on the bars of her cell that let her phase through them. An alarm began to blare, but no one showed up as Alma made her way randomly through the Cosmos Guardians' headquarters. The reason for this, quite simply, is they couldn't agree on how to stop her. They'd done their research on their target and knew that even a short conversation with her could change people's attitudes. Their metal dolls were supposed to work on her, a fighting force without mercy. Yet they hadn't, and so, a furious debate raged in the prisoner containment room. It involved a lot of yelling, since, being fascists, they believed that whoever shouts loudest and longest is right.

Alma found herself in a long corridor with prison cells on either side. The cells were filled with a similar sort of nasty-looking folks she'd met on the prison ship.

"You there," called out a man with dark skin, or probably dark skin as every inch of him had a tattoo of something scary and mean. "You're not one of them."

"I most certainly am not," said Alma.

"Can you get us out of here?"

"I could yes, but I'll only do so if you promise not to be bad. I don't know the criteria of how they imprison people around here, but I'd like some reassurance if I'm to start freeing people."

"Yeah, OK, I promise."

"Do you mean it?"

"I do."

"'Cause it's not a real promise unless you mean it."

"I … um."

"And I'll be real sad if you break your promise to me. You don't want to make me sad do you?"

"OK, I promise, I won't be bad."

"I believe that one."

So, after securing several promises from inmates to be on their best behavior, Alma started a prison riot. Which I know sounds bad, but remember, this is a fascist prison. It's always OK to riot in those.

With prisoners rioting at an increasing rate of about one every sincere promise, the prisoner command center entered into a state of panic. They did not act, however, since all they did was shout even louder.

By the time General Nitrel showed up, who could shout with the best of them, and restored some order to the prison command, most of the prison section of the Cosmos Guardians' headquarters was rioting. With calm restored at prison command General Nitrel determined the best course of action was to send the officers in with earplugs.

It's important to remember, of course, that all fascists are fundamentally cowards and only ever prefer fighting people helpless to defend themselves. These officers had signed up for the position thinking they'd never have to do any actual fighting. One of the things fascists are most afraid of, however, is that other people will realize they're cowards. The only people they manage to fool in this matter are themselves, but they're too stupid to know any better.

The officers marched down the halls while engaging in a contest of who could seem the most eager to fight while not actually being the first ones to engage in the fight. It involved a lot of shouting, bragging and insults mostly, while brandishing their weapons. People regularly edged to the back of the group while shouting very loudly about how they'd show these prisoners what it meant to mess with them. They sure couldn't wait to be the first to show those prisoners what for, they'd shout while patting someone else on the back to shove them just a little bit ahead.

You might be thinking, weren't they wearing earplugs? Why all the shouting?

As I said, they're stupid, and much of their performance was for themselves. Eventually, after "accidentally" losing their way a few times, the officers came upon the rioting prisoners.

A few in the front screamed, "Charge!" and went right for it. Those a bit further back thought it best to assess the situation and began to discuss tactics, or did what they considered discussing tactics, which was to loudly explain what they thought best and expect everyone else to listen. Those in the rear, concerned they'd look like the cowards they were, also screamed, "Charge!" and promptly ran into those in the middle.

What followed cannot in any good grace be called a battle. That said, the Cosmos Guardians lost this one badly.

Nothing is quite as intolerable to fascists as failure. So they called it a victory, and congratulated themselves on managing to prevent 100 percent of prisoners from escaping the terminal care wing of the hospital unit.

Among those who were capable of mobility, only two prisoners did not make it out of the prison.

Alma, like last time, let everyone else escape first. On the last shuttle off the station, as people rushed on board, Alma waited at the open door for the last person to enter. Once they did, she shouted for them to take off. The last prisoner on board the shuttle grabbed her, and jumped off the shuttle just before it took off out of the hangar bay. This prisoner being the same engineer who'd noticed the missing parts thinking he could free himself.

"What the hell?" Alma said after she'd gotten to her feet. "Why would you do that?"

"This is the only way I'll get my job back," the engineer said.

"If you work for them then why were you in prison?"

"I noticed the parts missing from the drones and they accused me of stealing them, but I know you did it."

"Yeah, I did. Why would you still want to work for people who falsely imprisoned you?"

The engineer stood up straight and straightened his prison garb. "I am a loyal Cosmos Guardian. We protect people in countless universes."

"Really? 'Cause it seems to me you mostly just harass innocent people and then occasionally imprison someone who may or may not be guilty."

At this point a group of officers burst into the hangar, several tripping over each other to try and apprehend Alma. A few grabbed her at once, each trying to shout the loudest that they were the ones who apprehended her.

Once again, it took General Nitrel to enter the room and restore some order. He had to shout especially loud this time because all the officers were wearing earplugs.

"Gag her," he said on seeing Alma. "GAG HER!" he shouted when no one heard him the first time. Several officers took some decorative handkerchiefs that they believed made them look classy (they didn't) and stuffed one into Alma's mouth.

"I'll be honest," Nitrel began his evil monologue, though it's worth noting he did not see himself as evil. "You've given us more trouble than I expected. We never did manage to detect what sort of magic it is that you use to get people to listen to you, but I thought our soldiers would be uniquely suited to overcome it. It seems, somehow, your magic worked on even them. Our plan was to use you as bait for your mother, then let you go. Yes, that's right, we were never after you, but your mother is too powerful to contend with. We knew we could never capture her, but once she had a child, finally a weakness presented itself. If we could get her to come to us we can set up a trap. Yet now you've orchestrated not one, but two prisoner escapes. It seems you'll be staying with us a while."

Alma let out a muffled laugh.

"Oh, you think that's funny do you? We'll see how funny it is twenty years from now. As for you." He turned to the engineer who stood up straight. "I saw on the camera you prevented her escape. It seems you were innocent after all, we'll take that into account at your sentencing."

"Sentencing?" The engineer looked puzzled.

"Yes, you did escape from prison yourself. The law must be obeyed."

"But, I didn't—"

"The law must be obeyed! Take them away!" No one moved. "I SAID TAKE THEM AWAY! AND TAKE THOSE THINGS OUT; SHE'S GAGGED, YOU IDIOTS!"

The collection of officers fumbled their earplugs out and, as a group, escorted the two prisoners back to Alma's cell. They might have noticed that they weren't supposed to put both prisoners in the same cell, but they were far too busy shouting at each other how no one could possibly hold any of them responsible for the whole affair while also talking about how it really was a victory if you think about it. They'd done their duty, and they made sure anyone walking by, which no one did on account of the prison being empty, knew.

CHAPTER 17

The Final Stop is a combination hotel, gas station, restaurant, casino, and children's theme park. It is often called the station at the center of the cosmos; this is inaccurate for two reasons. One, it isn't, and two, the cosmos, like a triangle, has multiple centers.

The name came more from it being the most popular place for people to stop when traveling in the spaces between. It was founded and run by Demensios, a creature of unknown origin and even more unknown motivation.

A series of intertwining circles drifted in and out of reality and space; the station hung on the edge of a destroyed universe. Ships shifted into the area and drove the rest of the way to one of the docks.

As usual, and to save on budget if this story ever gets adapted into live action, most of the visitors were some form of human or humanoid. Not everything, as blobs and multi-limbed monstrosities made their way among the series of rings larger than some planets. Creatures of more than three dimensions moved in and out of view.

Fights sometimes broke out among the bars, but Demensios himself quickly handled such things. Often those involved were never heard from again.

The *RainbowDeath* emerged from the void, its interdimensional engines blazing an array of colors appropriate to its name. Once the transition completed, the sublights kicked in and carried it to The Final Stop where it docked on one of the circles.

Jack Stallion stretched his limbs upon completing the journey. He flipped on the intercom. "We have arrived at our destination, everyone. If Honey and Melissa could please report to the bridge."

Melissa showed up a short while later, her wings scraping the ceiling and turning it a golden red as she moved. "I can't find Honey."

Jack swiveled in his captain's chair. "Really? You two have been together pretty much the whole trip."

"Yeah, she went out to eat and didn't come back."

Jack hit the intercom again. "Has anyone seen Honeydrops on board?"

A response came through. "She's passed out in the mess hall."

Jack and Melissa traveled to the mess hall where they found Honey passed out in a mixture of breadcrumbs and water. Alteem sat watch over her in a nearby chair with a cup of tea in his hand. He raised it in greeting when they entered.

"Is she OK?" Melissa knelt down next to her and placed a hand on her cheek.

"Yeah," Alteem said. "She's fine, just tired. I thought about waking her, but I was afraid she'd refuse to rest if I did."

"This is all my fault." Melissa gently shook Honey. "Baby, wake up."

Honey stirred, her eyes opening. She propped herself up on her side in a sexy pose with wet breadcrumbs falling off of her. "Oh, hey, Melissa. Ready for more?"

"I'm sorry, I overdid it. We've just been having so much fun."

"No, what? We haven't overdone it. I'm good for two to three hundred more times."

"Can you stand?"

"Am I not standing?"

Melissa shook her head.

"That's fine, I'll just crawl back to our bedchambers where we can continue our escapades. If I pass out again just keep going; I don't mind."

"Honey, you need a break."

"I do not, I'm the queen of sex. I can keep up with anybody." Honey's arm flopped in an attempt at a determined gesture. "Besides, we could always use more fuel."

Jack knelt down on her other side. "We actually have more than enough fuel at this point."

"Shut up, Jack, no one asked you."

"We've also arrived."

"Why didn't anybody say so?" Honey attempted to stand but only managed to flop around like a fish on dry land. "You may need to carry me."

Melissa scooped Honey up in her arms. "We can wait."

"No," Honey said, her head flopping against Melissa's shoulder. "My daughter is out there and it's already taken too long to get here. We're going now. I'm just going to take a quick nap."

Melissa carried the sleeping Honey out of the ship and onto The Last Stop. Jack and Max followed behind. As soon as Melissa set foot on the station a form appeared before them. Three electric eyes hung in distorted space.

"Is it really her?" a high-pitched voice echoed around them. "I've heard tales of the one they call the Witch, but never has she visited my humble establishment. Allow me to welcome you here at … is she asleep?"

"Sorry." Melissa swayed Honey a little like a baby. "We've been, uh, busy with important things and she's just exhausted."

Demensios's eyes narrowed in annoyance. "Then our meeting shall have to wait until after she's rested. Perhaps I could offer you a complimentary room."

"She could rest aboard our ship if that's what we wanted," Jack said. "We're here for information. We'll get it and we'll go."

Demensios's eyes nearly formed a smile. "If that's what you wish then I shall not stand in your way." The form disappeared into the air.

"I do not get a good feeling about that thing," Max said.

"We'll go to one of the bars." Jack took the lead in front. "If we're to find information about the Cosmos Guardians we'll find it there."

He led them past the refueling station, a place that displayed pictures of all manner of fuels, liquids, solids, and gases of all colors and consistencies. Some were pictures of light and a couple of abstract concepts.

They arrived at a bar with an even more diverse array of substances, though with a different purpose; some did serve double duty depending on a person's biology. This particular bar had dim lighting and a half circle for a counter with circular tables and stools. Red paint covered their surfaces, but it'd been worn away and never repainted so the metal beneath could be seen on the edges and through scratches.

Not much grabbed the attention of the interuniversal travelers, but a large angel carrying a famous witch turned some heads.

A thin, pale man with pink and purple spiked hair approached them at the entrance. He opened up his coat to reveal several vials with sparkling powder of different colors inside. "Wanna buy some pixie dust?"

Honey stirred. "Ooh, pixie dust." She reached for the vials, but Melissa pulled away.

"No, you know how you get."

"But it'll give me energy."

"I said no!"

Honey mumbled something before passing out again.

Melissa and Max approached the bar with Jack joining them a moment later. "I'm Max Stallion, this is Jack Stallion, no relation, and this is Melissa and Honey."

The bartender eyed Honey. "She looks like she's had enough."

Melissa hefted Honey. "She's not drunk; she's just exhausted from … activities."

"Right then, what'll you have?"

"We're not here for beverages; we're here for information."

"That's more expensive."

Jack put a coin on the table and slid it over. "We need to know the location of the Cosmos Guardians."

The bartender didn't take the coin. "Never heard of 'em, might try somewhere else. I don't even know how many bars are on this station."

"Thanks, anyway." Jack left the coin and they searched the bars of The Final Stop for anyone who might know anything. The bars were as varied as anything else in the cosmos. Some for aquatics were either entirely or mostly underwater. Melissa could not enter those since she'd make the water boil, but she alone entered those meant for demons whose floor ran molten. Some were high-class with people in fancy suits and dresses, and others were strip clubs with people taking off their clothes.

No one had any useful information for them. Demensios appeared before them once again. "No luck I take it?"

"Why are you so interested in Honey?" Melissa asked.

"Oh, so that's her name, absolutely delicious. How could I not be interested in her? She's said to be one of the few creatures more powerful than myself, and she's only human. Rare do I encounter such a thing."

"What do you want?" Jack asked.

"My hope was to be able to converse with her; pity that's impossible. I may be of assistance. We do have a travel directory that might help you find your way."

Melissa looked down at Honey, who currently had a small amount of drool pooling in the corner of her mouth. "I am nearly as powerful myself. Don't think I'd let you harm her."

Demensios's distortion loomed large in the air. "What a fool I would be to try and combat someone more powerful than myself. Is it not wiser to have someone more powerful owe you a favor?"

Max gave a reassuring nod to Melissa. "Nothing can hurt her."

Melissa shook her head. "That's not true; most things can't hurt her. I have known her longer than you and seen her push too many limits. I will not lose her now that I finally have her."

"We're not about to let anything happen to her. Trust me, I'm not about to let anyone kill her when I couldn't."

"I have no wish to offend, human, but you were hardly a match."

135

"Right …"

They followed the distortion as it led them through the winding walks of The Last Stop. Demensios's form gave little away as it floated along the path. If it were possible to read the motivations of such a thing, those present lacked the craft.

The room it took them to had a circular shape, with a series of consoles with black screens lined in an uneven pattern. Some were too big, others too small, with random spacing between them.

"Peruse as you wish." Demensios vanished as the words echoed in the chamber.

Max went over to one of the consoles. "These buttons aren't in any language I recognize." He pressed one and the screens around them hummed to life in a blinding white. The walls around them shifted like a living creature and the consoles shifted with them until a different one presented itself in front of Max. It dimmed to a dull blue and text in digital font appeared on the screen.

"What is your query?"

The keys were blank. He touched one and recoiled shaking his hand. "Burns!"

"It won't burn me." Melissa handed Honey over to Jack and approached the console.

"Wait," Max said. "Seems convenient to me you're the only one who can touch the keys?"

"Now you suspect a trap?"

"Never said I didn't, just said we wouldn't let harm come to her. You're the strongest person here who's conscious. If he set a trap for anyone it would be you."

Melissa examined the console, then pulled her molten blade from the air. "Let's see then." She slashed the console, and it split in where the blade touched it. The edges of the cut glowed hot, until they shifted and closed up. Then the walls around them began to shrink.

The angel's wings extended outward to their full glory. "Duck," she told her companions, and they did so. She spun around, her wings cutting into the walls as they closed around them. Then she flapped them, and white light exploded outward from her, hitting the slice in the walls and bursting them apart. She took her blade and cut through the edges of the wall in case it thought of reforming.

The walls fell away around them, and they stood on open air, the space around them distorted.

Melissa did not hesitate. She thrust her blade toward the distortion and golden flame shot forth. The distortion evaporated like air before the flame and Melissa unleashed it all around them, hitting the distortion where it appeared.

They found themselves standing on air in blackness.

"That was painful," Demensios's voice said. "Most painful, but sometimes pain is necessary for knowledge. You're as strong as you said, but ..."

A shackle appeared in the air and clasped itself around Melissa's wrist, her sword vanishing. It pulled her to the ground even as she strained against it.

Demensios appeared before them, three eyes in a distortion. "Forgive me, forgive me, I do so hate to be rude to my guests, but I've never had an angel come here before. Demons by the scores, but angels prefer to stay in their heavens. Such data I could never collect under normal circumstances. I'd hoped you'd use the console; easier that way, but getting you to use your power worked just as well. Even if you've done considerable damage to me. Couldn't have taken much more of that, but I've tuned into the, let's call it, frequency of your divine power now."

Melissa pulled up from the ground, and nearly pried the shackle off her wrist, but Demensios's distortion increased. For a second the two battled an invisible battle of wills that ended when the shackle pulled Melissa back to the ground.

"You are strong indeed; I can't sweat, but I would if I could. I must request you stay awhile. I wouldn't, I shouldn't; we work so hard on our reputation here, but who knows how long it will be before I have another opportunity to study an angel, if ever."

Max pulled out his ray gun and began firing at Demensios to no effect.

"You really think that would work on me? Ha. Ha. Ha. That thing might be advanced to you, but it may as well be a child's toy against myself."

Jack pulled out a vial from his pocket and sprinkled some pink dust into Honey's drooling mouth.

She popped up to her feet. "Fucking hell, that's a rush."

Demensios's distortion disappeared. "Unfortunate, but calculated for. You're not the first magic user I've encountered."

Another shackle appeared in the air and clasped around Honey's wrist.

"The pink stuff is my favorite, by the way. Thanks for that, Jackie boy."

"Damn it, Jack," Melissa said. "Did you have to use the pink stuff?"

"The guy said it was the strongest," Jack said with a shrug.

Honey started rubbing at her clothes. "We should all have sex, right the fuck now."

"We're in the middle of a fight with Demensios," Max said.

"That's even better; middle-of-a-fight sex is awesome."

Max holstered his ray gun. "I still don't want to have sex with you."

"Jack, how 'bout it?"

"Never," Jack said.

"You can't give a girl pink pixie dust and then not fuck her; that's just rude."

"Sorry?"

"Melissa?"

Melissa tried to stand again, but couldn't. "Honey, I'm shackled to the floor."

"When's that ever stopped us?"

"Demensios did this, to trap me."

"Without your consent? That son of a bitch. Wait, who's Demensios?" Another shackle appeared and clasped to Honey's other hand. "Where do these keep coming from? I'd say it's sexy, but without the rattling of chains it just doesn't quite hit right. Also I'm not wearing the right outfit for it. You know, I need to be showing more skin. Maybe a latex bra—uncomfortable, but a good deal of sexy things are."

Demensios spoke. "This is not possible; I've calculated the requirements for magic users millions of times. Why is it not working on you?"

"The whole point of magic is about doing things that aren't possible. I'd call it a wild untamable force, but it's not really a force. It's about grabbing reality by the throat and then choking that bitch until she does what you want. The whole point is breaking the rules, so there really aren't any rules. Don't get me wrong; you gotta be careful. Things can go terribly wrong, I mean look at my hair. There are consequences to messing up. Anyway, I'm the best at it in the whole damn cosmos and I'm so horny. That pink stuff, man, my loins are hot enough for fusion right now. Feels like I might be about to give birth to a star."

"Honey, focus, please," Melissa said.

"Really, you're lying there helpless and hot as fuck and you expect me to focus. I could barely focus in this situation if I wasn't on energy sex drugs. I keep looking down expecting a wet spot to form on my dress. I don't even think that's physically possible, but it sure as hell feels like it is right now."

"What is wrong with you?" Demensios asked.

"Holy shit! If that isn't the question of the goddamned millennia. What the hell is wrong with me? I'd usually go into my childhood right now and all the abuse I got from my mother, but lately I'm starting to think I'm just broken. Like, maybe some people are just broken from the start. It wouldn't have mattered if I had a great mother; I'd still be this fucked-up mess that I am. I have what I need right? People who care about me, a family, someone I love who loves me back. I'm the piece of the puzzle that doesn't fit, that can't fit. Nothing is ever gonna fix me, because this is the way I am. We just met, and you can already tell I'm not OK. Granted, I'm drugged up right now so it's not the best circumstances, but you'd still know even if I wasn't. I'm just, there's something wrong with me and everyone knows it, but they have to put up with me anyway because here I am."

Demensios did not frown, but it rather looked like he did. "I've met some of the most powerful and incredible creatures in all the cosmos, and at last I've met you, the most powerful of them all. I must say my disappointment is immeasurable. You are without grace, dignity, or even the slightest bit of poise. Powerful as you are, you're trash."

"Wow, well if you're gonna fuck someone in the ass like that at least use a little lube. Maybe some clit action or a reach-around depending. I'm sorry, that was a terrible metaphor; it's the drugs ... it's mostly the drugs. Who even are you?"

"I'm Demensios, you idiot. Who else would I be?"

"Right, that does make sense given the context clues. You shackled my girlfriend without her consent. I've been trying really hard not to kill anyone for almost two decades now, but you've crossed a line."

"Your magic has been studied and calculated; there's little you can do to me—"

Honey flexed her hand, the shackles shattered. The distorted form of Demensios twisted and bent as a purple vine of neon energy snaked its way around him. The blackness fell away and they stood on the space station once more.

"You seem like a smart guy." Honey examined her nails. "I'm not sure what it is about the most powerful person in the cosmos you don't understand. Maybe if you had a couple of friends, you'd stand a chance. Even the strongest fighter can be taken down by a sufficient mob, but alone? Because of what? Calculations? You can't calculate magic; it's indefinable. It just means doing shit that isn't possible. I don't know if this is getting through to you at all?"

"Do as you will," Demensios said. "You are still human, and I am beyond your comprehension."

"You know how many beings said that to me before I destroyed them? You think I can't feel every part of you, spread through this space station, across several dimensions." The space station shuddered and shook. "I can wrench you apart, and if I can't get laid then I'll be happy with some old-fashioned mass destruction."

Demensios's voice came grasping and distorted. "You pathetic creature. A preening, self-loathing mess of insecurity does not deserve such power."

"No shit. Since when have the people who deserved power gotten it? Now die."

"Honey, stop!" Melissa wrenched against the shackle once more; with Demensios being torn apart it came undone. The angel wrapped herself around her lover, enfolding them both in the light of her wings. "There are tens of thousands of people aboard this station. If you destroy it, they'll die."

Honey squeezed; the station shuddered, and Demensios's eyes turned into a smile. "You should listen to your girlfriend."

Melissa ran a hand along the side of Honey's face. "You are not that person anymore?"

Honey's eyes started to blaze purple. "Aren't I? Maybe that's all I am, all I'll ever be. What if I'm just fooling myself into thinking I can be more than that?"

"No, I know you. That's not you; it never was. Other people put all that inside of you."

"You're wrong; I am the broken thing that ruins." She squeezed more and cracks formed in the station. In the distance people could be seen panicking and fleeing toward their ships.

"Stop it! You've never ruined me. My life is better because of you. You said you wouldn't push me away anymore, so don't."

Honey relaxed her hand, and the station went still again. "Won't have sex with me, won't let me destroy things. You're awful."

"You'll be OK, you just need to ride out the drugs."

Honey let out a disgruntled moan, then sank to the floor, out of Melissa's arms. "This is bullshit."

Demensios's form escaped the purple vine of energy. "That's much better, isn't it?"

Melissa flew toward him and grappled him with her wings. "Still weak, are you?"

"Indeed, but you lack the strength to do little but hold me."

"Oh, a little more than that." Melissa twisted the being in her wings.

"That does indeed hurt, but why hurt me?"

"I don't like my girlfriend being drugged. Me and Jack will have a talk later, but for now, we came here for information. You promised us that information and then led us into a trap."

"Nice recap on something that just happened."

Melissa's wings twisted further. "Give us the information, or I will wring you out so badly you won't be able to properly manifest for a thousand years."

"Torture is not an effective method for extracting information."

"Let's add to the data then."

"No need, no need. I've gotten plenty of information to make this all worth my while. I shall give you the coordinates to the Guardians of the Cosmos. Then we can all part ways as friends." A console appeared behind them with a five-point dataset. Three points for coordinates in three-dimensional space. One point for the universe, another for the specific reality.

Melissa gave Demensios a good twist, where his form bent and shrank. Then she let him go and he disappeared.

"Highly unnecessary." His voice echoed away.

CHAPTER 18

Alma and the engineer resided in her cell.

"How have you managed to organize two mass escapes where you're the only person who didn't escape?" the engineer asked.

"Tell me about it. Needless to say you won't be included in my next escape attempt on account of you stabbing me in the back, metaphorically speaking." Alma began poking at the parts of her cell she'd escaped through before.

"I did my job."

Alma looked over at the engineer who sat down in the middle of the cell. "How's that working out for you? Honestly, what did you expect joining a fascist organization? They always eat their own."

The engineer threw his hands up and scoffed. "Of course, play the fascist card. Look, just because people do all the things fascists do, doesn't make them fascist. The real fascists are the people who oppose fascism. If you see someone out there trying to stop a fascist, then you know they're a fascist."

"Wow, just coming out and saying it straight up like that. Normally people try and dress up their nonsense a bit more than that."

The engineer began to nod aggressively. "It's not nonsense; everything I'm saying is perfectly logical because it makes sense to me.

That's what logic is: when someone says something, and you like it so you agree with it."

"You're the most self-aware fascist toady I've ever met, I'll give you that."

"You're just relying on insults because you're stupid. If you were smart you wouldn't need to use insults."

"Uh-huh." Alma turned back to the bars of her cell. "If you'll excuse me I have to once again figure out how I'm going to get out of here."

"If you do, I'll just tell on you again."

"I don't think that'll be a problem: fascist don't hold the words of criminals in high regard, except the ones leading them."

"I am NOT a criminal!" The engineer pounded his fist on the ground like a child. "I'm a good person."

"Those two things are not mutually exclusive, and you are the opposite of your claims."

"I see, now you're using big words to try to confuse me. Well, I'll have you know I memorized a sentence of big words for just such an occasion."

"Could you use any of those memorized words outside of that sentence?"

"Probably."

"Then do it."

"Um, the defenestration was very defenisitive."

"Right."

The engineer's face started to turn red. "Well you're a criminal too."

"Everyone is somewhere." Alma pushed a hand through one of the bars.

"What?"

"We've all done something that's illegal somewhere. Everyone is a criminal in some part of the cosmos. Most people don't even need to go outside of their home planets to be a criminal somewhere."

"I'm not, and I never will ever break any law ever."

"See I don't think you're stupid; I think you'll just say whatever you have to in order to avoid being wrong. To you, it's not about what's right; it's about being right."

"No, no, I'm totally wrong right now."

"I want you to think about what you just said."

"If I wanted to stop and think about things I wouldn't be where I am today." The engineer crossed his arms and turned away from Alma.

"OK, yup, that's right."

"Then you admit that the Cosmos Guardians are not fascist." He held up a finger in triumph.

"Nope, being right about one thing doesn't make you right about any other thing."

"I choose to see it differently."

Alma traced a hand across the floor. "It doesn't seem like they've done much to undo what I did last time, so I think I can just teleport out again. Not sure how I'll get off the station from here, but given the guards are on my side I think I can stow away for a good while."

"What, but you can't." The engineer reached for Alma; though sitting on the floor he didn't get very far.

"I can though." Alma's form shimmered in the air and phased through the bars of the cell. "You see it doesn't matter what you want to be true; what matters is what is true. Try to remember that in the future and you'll be much happier."

"Guards, somebody stop her." No one came.

"Guess fascists aren't interested in the words of a criminal." Alma walked out of the room leaving the engineer alone.

Later an officer would come to the cell to deliver some food since drones had been deemed unreliable in the delivery of food.

The engineer grabbed the bars of his cell. "She's escaped; you have to find her."

"Please back away from the cell, inmate," the officer said.

"But, she's out there."

"Who?"

"The witch's daughter. The most important prisoner we've ever had, that's who."

"I think we'd know if such an important prisoner had escaped." The smugness of the officer's voice cannot be overstated. He held up his pad. "It says right here there's supposed to be one prisoner in this cell, and behold, there is only one."

"But, but, doesn't it also say that it's supposed to be the witch's daughter?"

"Yes it does, which means this clearly must be some sort of ruse. I think you'll find we're much too smart to fall for that sort of trickery here, witch. Now if you don't back away from the bars you'll get no food."

"Goddamn it, Jeff, you know me. I was at your sister's wedding. We played poker together every third Wednesday of the month."

"No food it is then." The officer left the room with tray in hand.

The engineer sunk to the floor, and did his best not to cry. In this he mostly succeeded. He did what all fools do when they cannot handle the reality before them and tried to turn his sorrow into anger.

Alma found she had free roam about the space station. One officer did see her, but concluded that she couldn't possibly be there if she wasn't supposed to be there. After all, their security is the best security in the world; therefore no one could just wander around unless they were allowed to wander around. Since Alma very obviously wasn't allowed to wander around, she couldn't be wandering around and therefore, could not be.

The perfect soldiers of the cosmos recognized Alma whenever she held their hands, and did not impede her. Getting off the station proved, thus far, impossible. The procedure for incoming and outgoing vessels remained strict and without an army of rioting prisoners she couldn't take them over. Instead she started playing games with the soldiers.

Yes, of course, the soldiers had all of their senses fed to them by their suits, which were controlled by the officers.

146

Alma planned and schemed for a few days to steal one of the pads, but after weighing her options she came up with a bold strategy. She walked up to one of the officers sitting at their desks, swiped the pad and walked away. The reasoning being that such a thing was so absurd that it couldn't possibly have happened at all. Sure enough, it worked.

The ultimate soldiers of the Cosmos Guardians went about their days playing games with Alma. The officers aboard did notice something different going on with their army, but since something couldn't be wrong with the perfect army, it therefore wasn't.

CHAPTER 19

Honey rode out the remainder of the drugs aboard the *RainbowDeath*. Mostly during this time she complained about being denied orgasm. Sure, she'd be OK with it as part of a kink thing, but not because if she did orgasm it would make the drugs worse. Melissa remained steadfast, and when the drugs wore off Honey collapsed into an exhaustion even worse than before.

Melissa did not like leaving her lover alone in their bed, but she needed to talk to one Jack Stallion.

"I did it to save us," he said sitting in his pilot's chair, his feet up on the console. "If I hadn't you'd be a prisoner and I don't think he'd have spared the rest of us. He wouldn't let Honey regain consciousness knowing she'd come after you."

"If you have to resort to drugging Honey, then you're not much of a hero." Melissa's eyes turned a bright molten gold.

"I'm sorry, I didn't know the pink stuff was a sex drug; I asked around and I now know I should've gotten the green stuff."

"That's not the point; you shouldn't have drugged her at all."

"We had to do something." Jack turned his back to the angel and focused on the console.

"I thought you were better than this. She is not some tool for you all to use at your convenience."

"So I should have let that guy take you and kill the rest of us?"

"I wasn't done fighting."

"You looked pretty beaten to me, and me and Max are nowhere near as powerful. When you're not all powerful your options are more limited. It's not something someone like you would understand, being a divine being. Nor would you understand what it's like to watch those you're supposed to save die. I wasn't about to sit back and let everything fall apart again. It's both of your faults we ended up in that situation anyway."

"I …" Melissa slumped, her wings heating the metal below her. "I didn't know she'd gone so far. Why did she do that?"

"Because she wants to keep you around."

"I've told her over and over again I'm not going anywhere. I'm here to stay."

"You two have a long history that I don't know much about, but, it's not so easy to believe that patterns can just be ended like that. I know for you it's the truth, but she's used to people not liking her and leaving."

"You're more insightful than I expected, Jack."

Jack stopped toying with the console. "It can be easier to understand people you have stuff in common with. Honey and I both have a lot of experience with failure."

"What does she need?"

"I'd say therapy, but I don't know if there's enough of that. If one could quantify therapy into liters, I'd say she needs several oceans' worth. Several planets' worth of oceans."

"What's therapy? I will find oceans of it no matter how rare."

"Uh … well, it's more a type of … mental medicine treatment where you sit down in a room with a qualified professional and work out what's wrong with you."

"I see, so if I want to help Honey I should find several oceans' worth of these individuals?"

"We've never really talked, just the two of us, and it's sinking in for the first time how much of a human you aren't." Jack resumed his work on the console.

"I confess, my lack of understanding of mortals is often an obstacle for me."

"I don't want to cross any boundaries, but you two seem mismatched."

"My life began when I met Honey; before that I didn't live I just existed. I think most angels are like that. We're born to be living tools of our gods, but Honey opened me up to things I'd never have dreamed of experiencing. In fact, before Honey I never dreamed of anything."

"Just because Honey opened you up that doesn't mean you two are right for each other. Sometimes two people can desperately want to be together, and still not make things work."

"I'm a field without rain when she's not around." Melissa closed her eyes and turned her head away with a pained expression. "Then she comes, and the flowers bloom again. It's not always easy, but she makes me want to be more than I am. I dream of a future when she's around, and when she's not, I'm standing still."

Jack turned around in his seat. "I don't really know what do with that."

"I so often feel like I need her, but I'm not sure she needs me. Others reached her when I couldn't. What if the best thing I can do for her is to leave her alone? What if I'm just holding back the person who is everything to me? The longest time we were apart she became a better person."

"If she is everything to you, why did you keep leaving?"

"Because I could not bear to watch her keep making the same mistakes. Now she's making all new ones and I find myself powerless to help. Loving someone is not enough to save them, no matter how much love you have."

"I know that lesson well. Love does not save people, no matter how much we insist it does."

"What does?"

Jack's eyes glanced down at the heating metal beneath the angel's wings. "Ask me before I met Honey, and I would've said power. Hasn't done her any fucking good though has it? Who knows what we need?"

"There is no suffering in my universe. I won a war to end evil for people who meant nothing to me. It's what I was made for. I do not know how to grant that same happiness to the person I love. Striking down an evil god seems so easy compared to the complex lives you mortals live."

"It's not as easy for the rest to just beat the bad guy and fix everything."

"Perhaps you're the wrong person to talk to about this. I should seek other counsel."

"Great, thanks for that. Nice talking to you." Jack returned to monitoring the course of the *RainbowDeath*.

"Yes, don't drug Honey ever again."

"In the future let's do a better job of never making it necessary."

Melissa gave Jack a nod and went searching for someone with more knowledge of the situation. A man who spent most of his time in the canteen.

Alteem sat, as usual, drinking some tea and talking with people when Melissa approached him.

"Can you tell me what happened?" she asked Alteem.

"About?" Alteem said.

"How did Honey become good?"

"Oh that, well, it's a bit of a story. A bit over sixty thousand words I'd say. Actually it started closer to seventy thousand but certain parts needed to be cut out for pacing reasons. We met a cult that worshipped me, but, really it didn't add much to the central theme of the story and I just felt it dragged things down bit. There's also a section about the insect people, but it didn't have much to do with Honey and most of what it did cover was covered better elsewhere."

"There must have been something important that happened to change her so much."

"It all happened a little at a time. Honestly when I think back to who she was compared to who she became, she's not the same person. Yet, she only changed a bit here, and a bit there. I think that's the way it usually happens for everyone. There aren't massive moments that define us, but little things along the way. Hell I'm not the same person I was when we met. For one thing I've learned to roll a lot better with the crazy shit." Alteem tipped his tea toward her.

"I feel so helpless. I'm a battle angel; no one taught me how to navigate situations like this. I want to say the right thing to her, but I never seem to manage it."

"I think it's mostly that way for everyone. Sure sometimes you meet someone who from the outside appears put together, but I promise that's never the case. Don't feel bad if you don't always know the right thing to say. You're there for her; that'll get through in the end."

"You really think so?"

"Yeah. Things will probably get much crazier before then if history is any indication, but you two will make it."

"I wish I felt as certain as you sound."

Alteem set his now empty cup of tea on the table. "It's not you she has a problem with, but I'm not sure she can overcome that hurdle."

"Who does she have a problem with?"

Honey had the power to heal people magically, but with her being heavily passed out from exhaustion the ship had another doctor on board.

Mathew, with nothing better to do, watched his wife, Issa, examine the vitals of the passed-out witch.

"Her vitals," Issa said holding on to Honey's wrist, "remain perfect. It's eerie how perfect every aspect of her is."

"Other than her personality," Mathew added.

"Don't be unkind."

"Sorry, but you have to admit, she can be a bit much."

Honey's eyes snapped open, and she sat up looking around. "Did I pass out in the middle of another threesome?"

Issa let go of the witch's wrist. "No, I was simply monitoring your health while you rested. It's been two weeks now."

"Oh, what happened?"

Mathew stood up. "You passed out from sex drugs."

"That doesn't sound like me. I can handle my sex drugs."

"To be precise," Issa said gathering up her doctor's bag, "you passed out from exhaustion, then were briefly revived by sex drugs, only to pass out even more exhausted than before."

"That sounds a lot more like me." Honey stretched her arms in the air. "Did you two want to have another threesome?"

Mathew gave a long sigh. "You just woke up from sex exhaustion."

"Yeah, and I'm rested and ready to go."

"It's probably best you don't exert yourself too much," Issa said.

"Bummer." Honey hesitated a moment as she studied her hands. "Where's Melissa?"

"She's been reading up on a therapy."

"Oh, I thought maybe she left."

Mathew walked over and sat on the bed. "Why would she leave? She's a bit obsessed with you."

"She always leaves. She says she won't this time, but come on, you know how I am. I see her look away or wince every time I do or say something stupid. And I say to myself, stop saying stupid shit, Honey, but then I open my mouth and it just comes tumbling out of me. Why do I keep saying stupid shit, Mathew? Why do I keep saying stupid shit?!"

"I've been asking that question since we first met and I've yet to get an answer."

"I'm so sorry about coming back into your life. No one should have to put up with me, let alone twice."

"I'm actually glad we got to meet again."

Honey pulled away from the couple. "The hell you are."

"I haven't had the opportunity yet, but I wanted to say I'm sorry for how we left things last time. I wanted to thank you too; Mother really enjoyed her time with you and I'm glad she had that before the end."

Honey stared at Mathew for an awkward amount of time. "Are you on drugs?"

"It's funny; you used to have this mask of false narcissism that you wore to cover up your deep insecurity, and now all you have is the insecurity. Believe it or not, even before your transformation, you did good things in the world."

"Does it matter? I can't ever make up for everything I've done, Mathew. You understand, you hate me as much as anyone. And you're right, people should hate me."

"I don't hate you—"

"Don't say that."

"Sometimes I might want to strangle you, but—"

"You should have said something during the threesome. I'd absolutely let you choke me."

"But"—Mathew gave Honey a glare before continuing—"you can't just keep punishing yourself."

"But I deserve it. After all that I've done, can you honestly say that I should get to be happy?"

"Yes, honestly and easily."

Honey looked at Mathew as if she could not believe what he just said, a reversal of how things usually went. "You can't mean that. Someone like me doesn't get a happy ending."

"It's been a while, Honey, but I have gained some wisdom since we last met. I wish you'd told me about our daughter, but I understand you were afraid of losing the last bit of joy in your life. People are quick to jump to punishment and suffering when others commit wrongs. It's so easy to judge and become drunk on our own self-righteousness. In my work I've seen a lot of families torn apart, and Issa can tell you about the things she's seen. More than once I've held her as she cried herself to sleep. I realized the world you came into is a world where you were possible. There's always suffering and cruelty and selfishness. Cycles of pain and trauma, but sometimes someone comes along with the strength to break that trauma. We all inherit these cycles and they spin the world around in their heartache. I don't know what kind of cycle you inherited, and I can't absolve you of all you've done. But you broke that cycle; I've seen it in your daughter. Let yourself be happy, even if just a little bit."

Honey twisted her hands together. "I don't know how. I'm broken and running on pain, and if I stop I think I'll fall apart."

"OK, uh, I want to help you with that, but I don't know how."

"Yeah, me fuckin' neither."

"I don't know if it counts for much," Issa said, "but I don't believe people can be broken. Flawed yes, but flawed isn't broken. You might feel that way, but I think you're amazing."

"Not just physically?"

"Not just. Maybe you don't see it, but I understand why Melissa wants to be with you."

"That might be the best thing anyone's ever said to me."

"Also, once you've fully recovered, I wouldn't mind another threesome. Mathew?"

"Uh?" Mathew coughed.

"Yeah, we'd like to do it again, or maybe a few more times. If you want."

"Hey, Mathew." Honey punched him in the arm. "Looks like you'll get to choke me after all."

CHAPTER 20

Honey found Melissa reading a book near one of the windows on the ship. The window had a slight red tint to it and sometimes you could see the faint outline of someone screaming in it from the corner of your eye, but that's what happens when you build a ship out of hell metal.

Honey hugged her own arm as she approached her girlfriend. "Hey, Melissa."

Melissa looked up from the book, which had made for difficult reading since she had to read it with her gauntlets on or, ya know, it would burst into flames. "Honey, good, you're awake. I've been reading, and I think you've been using sex as a coping mechanism to avoid dealing with your issues."

"What?"

"Yeah, it's all in this book all about nymphomaniacs." Melissa held up the book, which was titled *A Book All About Nymphomaniacs.*

"Can't a girl just love sex?"

"Honey, you had sex until you passed out. I asked around, and you even had an orgy in the bathroom between two of our sessions."

"That orgy had already started; I just joined in."

"You can't keep going like this."

"So what, I'm just supposed to stop having sex? I already promised Mathew and Issa more threesomes. You want me to disappoint them?"

"I'm not saying you can't have any sex; you just need to learn to be aware of when you're doing it because you want to and when you're doing it to avoid your feelings."

"This is just like Louisa and Parnell."

Melissa put her book down. "True, and just like Louisa I think you use your bombastic personality as an excuse to avoid discussions you don't want to have."

"What the hell, Melissa?" Honey backed away. "I just woke up; I don't need to be attacked like this."

"I'm not attacking you; I'm trying to help you."

"Well I don't like it, and I'm leaving."

Melissa stood up. "Stop running away from all this."

"I'm not the one who runs away; that's you."

"Please not this again. I've told you I'm not leaving this time."

"I still feel like you will. I keep thinking it will go away with time, but it doesn't. Every time you make one of your faces I think I've done it again and it's all going to fall apart."

"Do you ever think I worry sometimes too? Not once have you ever come after me. I'm always the one who seeks you out. Why is that?"

"Because you're better off without me!"

The alarms on the ship began to blare.

"Seriously!" Honey screamed. The two marched to the bridge of the ship. "What now?"

Jack pointed at the giant creature taking up the field of view from the bridge. Its skin was tar with red rivers of corpses miles long running across it. Big enough to devour planets, its mouth was a gaping void that swallowed light. To stare at it induced voices whispering of the end of all things.

Its shape moved like a sea creature, expanding and collapsing as it floated in space. A skirt of flesh around its bottom expelled neon gases, which fizzed and exploded. Five eyes surrounded the mouth, each the size of a sun, but within them another eye, and another inside that eye.

A thousand eyes, each smaller than the last until the final eyes, all of which looked directly at the bridge of the ship.

"Fucking Dylan," Honey said. "What do you want?"

Nightmares invaded the minds of everyone on board the ship. Clips of broken terror, people on planets being devoured, the sensation of being eaten alive, being consumed by smells that eat you from the inside out.

"Don't start with me; I'm in no mood."

More images danced across the minds of everyone on board. Terrible sensations and images that left people clinging to each other.

"Yes, me and Melissa are back together; it's complicated. Why are you here?"

The images came once again.

"I'll take whatever tone I want. Remember Sheela's wedding? 'Cause I do, and no one has forgiven you."

A sensation: everyone falling, being pulled into nothingness.

"Now you're sorry. Please, it's only because you want something. So just spit it out."

Agony, a wrenching pain of something burrowing through your insides and mixing them up in the process.

"I'm not a doctor, Dylan."

Jack grabbed on to Honey. "Please, make it stop." He trembled as he held on to her.

"Right, right. Sorry, I can just." Honey took a dagger and pricked the edge of one of her fingers. Using her blood she smeared a symbol on the window of the bridge. The sensations stopped.

A voice came from the symbol, distorted and stretched thin. "Please, something is very wrong with me."

"Die then; see if I care. I guess even elder gods expire eventually."

"I am ... afraid to die."

"You don't think all the people you subsumed were afraid? You're a parasite, and everyone else is better without you around."

Melissa put a hand on Honey's shoulder. "We should help him."

"This is Dylan we're talking about, Melissa; fucking Dylan."

"I remember Sheela's wedding; I was your plus one. I think it would be good for you to help him."

"I don't know what you were reading, but you need to stop with this stuff."

Melissa enveloped Honey in a hug. "It's easy to help the ones who deserve it. You need to learn that even the ones who don't deserve it are worth helping. You're worth it."

Tears appeared at the edges of Honey's eyes. "But it's fucking Dylan."

"Remember when Louisa and Parnell had to help the Prince of Cortelais?"

"You're right." Honey sniffed. "But like I said I'm not a doctor. I'm not sure if I can help him."

"We do have a doctor on board," Jack said.

"No," Honey said. "No way; I'm not making Issa traipse through Dylan's innards. She's a good person with fun, pillowy breasts."

"It should be her decision, shouldn't it?" Melissa said.

They entered inside the incision together. The tar flesh closed behind them in seconds. Honey held up a purple orb to light in front of them while Melissa's wings lit behind them. Issa wore a yellow spacesuit, which fit her poorly. The chest and hips too tight with the shoulders and arms loose. Magic runes glowing in blood both human and angelic covered the suit to protect it from the foul forces inside Dylan.

In the air, gases floated by in neon colors. If any of them touched the gases, sparks ignited causing a small explosion. Honey's magic protected them, and Melissa's power eclipsed something as wimpy as an elder god.

"What exactly are we looking for?" Issa asked.

"Anything out of the ordinary," Honey said as a human skeleton walked by in a top hat. It tipped its hat to them and walked on.

"Is that unusual?"

"No, that happens every two to three minutes in here."

"I'm not sure I'm qualified for this job."

"I'll point it out if we encounter anything we shouldn't."

"How do you know about his insides?"

"Sheela's wedding," Honey and Melissa said at the same time. "Don't ask; it's a sore subject," Honey finished.

"OK," Issa said and they made their way deeper into the innards of an elder god. Veins of bloody corpses flowed past them. Creatures with rotting bodies scuttled about at the edges of the light. Every three minutes or so the skeleton walked by in his top hat, which it tipped toward them again.

The halls around them narrowed as they went deeper inside. The tar-like flesh grew thinner and they could see images of themselves walking on the other side of it. Their reflections showed them rotting and falling apart, only to be restored when they blinked and started to rot again. The skeleton said, "Excuse me," as it had to squeeze past in the narrower corridors before tipping its hat.

A chamber opened up before them; they could see several other corridors converging here. The walls were so black that they seemed to go on forever. At the center of the chamber a sphere of red flesh pulsed in inflamed colors. Hundreds of bunny ears protruded from the sphere.

"OK," said Honey. "The bunny ears are new; it used to be razor-sharp bones."

"My professional opinion as a doctor," said Issa, "is that I have no idea what to do about that."

The skeleton walked by again.

"Do you know why the skeleton does that?"

"Who cares?" Honey said. "Let's cut this baby open and see what's going on inside." The light in her hand turned into a sharp dagger as she approached the sphere.

"Will that hurt him?"

"Who cares? It's Dylan." Honey sliced open the sphere and more bunny ears poured out from inside it as the walls around them rumbled.

"Huh, bunny ears all the way down." She reached into the sphere and started pulling out more of the ears, but they did not stop.

The skeleton walked by once more, and this time Issa curtsied back to him. He stopped, his bones starting to glow white. The chamber began to shake and the glow grew brighter until the only thing that could be seen was the glow.

The elder god's flesh around them caught flame and burned away, and the skeleton shone so bright in the now bare air that many light-years from now planets around the area would see a new star for the few seconds it lasted.

The light vanished and in its place a man. His skin was a bright bronze, a circular hat on his head, blue on the upper half, white on the underside. His eyes were emerald, and his body muscular. A white cloth remained wrapped around his waist, tied in the front with the tassels hanging down.

"Thank you," he said. "I am Amuliashtin. Once I was a god who ruled over this now broken universe, but I made a foolish mistake that cursed me to be a skeleton wandering the stars until someone returned my polite gesture with another. My power leaked out of me and formed a cruel creature around me that did unspeakable things. You have broken my curse, and for that I will be forever indebted to you. Seek me out anytime you need anything. I must go now; I have much work to do restoring this universe. I shall be wiser this time, and learn from the arrogance that doomed all I had made."

Issa did not say anything until Honey nudged her. "OK," she said, her voice quavering in uncertainty.

The god vanished leaving the three hanging in space.

"Now we're never going to know what those bunny ears were about," Honey said.

CHAPTER 21

The *RainbowDeath* approached the headquarters of the Guardians of the Cosmos. The space station hung in space in bright, friendly red and blue colors. Ball-shaped, and made up of thousands of individual domes. Many of the domes were glass with green grass and vibrant flowers visible beneath. Children could be seen playing in these gardens. A space dock extended outward with flashing neon sign that said "Welcome" in an obnoxiously inviting font.

"Is it possible," said Jack Stallion, "we've come to the wrong coordinates?"

"The coordinates are right," said Max. "Maybe Demensios lied to us?"

Honey entered the bridge. "That's it then?"

"Well," the men said at the same time, "we think maybe—"

Purple flared up around the bridge. Honey strapped two tendrils and started to pull back on them.

"What are you doing?" Max asked.

"I'm gonna launch myself into their headquarters. Hopefully hitting something at comet speed."

"Through the windshield."

"Don't worry, I'll be fine."

"We won't be."

Honey looked at them. "Because … ?"

163

"The deadly vacuum of space."

"Right, I forgot that's a thing. Can you believe it? I just had this conversation with Issa too. OK, I'll launch myself out of the hangar then."

"Wait don't—," Jack started but Honey vanished out the door as quickly as she'd come.

Melissa arrived shortly after. "Where is she?"

"The hangar."

"How can someone so short run so fast?" Melissa grumbled as she followed after.

In the hangar Honey used her magic to push some shuttles out of the way so she could have a clear launch path to the headquarters. Melissa arrived to see her pulling back about to launch herself.

"Honey, stop!"

"They have my daughter; I am going to tear them apart," Honey said, her grip loosening on her tendrils.

"This might be a trap for you. They wouldn't have done this if they didn't have a way to stop you. Please, I know you think you have to take whatever punishment comes your way, but you're not alone. Let people help you."

"I'm sorry." Honey let go of the tendrils, and the power snapped her out of the hangar. Melissa dove after her at a much slower rate.

Honey flew through space in a tornado of neon purple. A whirl of power that grew bigger as she flew. People on the station noticed and began pointing at her. Someone had the foresight to turn on the shield, which absorbed the brunt of the human projectile that crashed into the lobby of the station.

The lobby had clean white floors with color-coded ribbons leading to different desks with different functions. The walls were covered with murals and children's drawings of family life. Honey picked herself off the crack she'd left in the floor, a torrent of violet colors flowing out of her. She grabbed the nearest person out of a desk with her power and lifted him to her face.

"May I help you?" the man asked in his blue suit.

"You will give me back my daughter," Honey said, smoke pouring out of her mouth as she spoke. "Or I will cut your dick off and feed it to you."

"I'd be happy to accommodate you, ma'am, but you must tell me who your daughter is first."

"Don't play with me." Honey's eyes blazed to life. "You know exactly who I am and why I'm here. You cop pieces of shit. You wanted me; here I am."

"Ah," the man said, unusually calm given his circumstances. "You must be looking for the Cosmos Guardians; we're the Guardians of the Cosmos."

"What?" Honey's eyes went back to their normal toxic green and the torrent of energy around her vanished. "You didn't kidnap my daughter in order to lure me into a trap?"

"No, I'm afraid not."

Honey put the man down and padded down his uniform where she'd ruffled it. "I'm really sorry about this."

"It happens more often than we'd like," the man said with a reassuring smile.

"I'm sorry about the floor, and the couple of walls I smashed through to get here."

"No problem at all really. We have nanites that'll repair at that in a couple of hours."

Honey looked around; many had fled on her arrival, while others remained frozen in fear. "I feel super bad; maybe there's something I can do to make up for it."

"You really don't have to. Like I said, you're hardly the first person to come through here seeking revenge against the Cosmos Guardians. Though, if you'd like, we've been working on our own cosmic database or CD; maybe you'd be willing to enter yourself."

"I suppose I better after all this trouble."

"No obligation, I assure you, completely voluntary."

"No, I better; what is it?"

The man led Honey over to his desk. "Well, you might have heard of a cosmonautical DNA database."

"Doesn't ring any bells."

"Well, they're databases containing the genetic makeup of every being who's ever existed in the universe. We've been trying to improve on that by adding more than just the genetic data. A bit of information about everyone who's ever existed. You can just provide us with information about yourself and we'll add it to the database."

Honey stopped walking. "How much information about myself?"

"As much as you'd like. We can even use a genetic sample to find out if you have any living relatives."

"I think I did want to do that."

"Excellent." The man sat at his desk. "Have a seat." Honey obliged as the man fetched a cheek swab. "Just use this for a sample of your DNA."

Honey reached down and started to lift up her skirt.

"No," the man said. "You can just use the inside of your cheek."

"Oh yeah." Honey put her skirt back down. "Of course." She swabbed the inside of her cheek and handed it back to the man who put it inside the chamber on his console.

"Let's see here," he said pressing some buttons. "Oh, well, we have three close matches. Interesting, seems all three are members of the Guardians of the Cosmos."

"Not at all what I expected, but ... good?"

"Our goal is to make the cosmos a better place. We used to just hunt and trap eldritch abominations, but we decided to expand our role. That's why we ended up splitting with the Cosmos Guardians. We both went in very different directions."

"So, about my relations?"

"Yes of course." The man adjusted his glasses and navigated his screen. "Unusual, says your father is one of them."

"What?" Honey's jaw became stiff and her eyes got wider.

166

"Yes, he's away on a terraforming mission. Actually looks like he's always away on terraforming missions. Strange you wouldn't know that."

"I was told my father is dead."

"Ah, well, he most certainly isn't. And your mother is right here living on the station. Looks like you have a half-sister with her new husband."

"I think there must be some sort of mistake." Honey's voice grew thin. "My parents are dead."

"Oh no, our systems are foolproof I assure you."

"Check it again."

"I can, but the results will be—"

"Check it the fuck again!" Honey broke off the edge of the desk.

"OK." The man pressed a few more buttons. "Yes, the results are the same."

Honey rose to her feet. "That's not possible."

"I can see this news is distressing for you, ma'am. Is there anything I can do?"

Honey said nothing, but her eyes became more intense and chaotic with each passing moment.

An angel flew in through the crack in the wall, looked around the room, spotted Honey and flew to her.

"Honey," Melissa said. "What happened? Is everything alright?"

"I'm going to kill her," Honey said, her voice cracking. Her eyes locked on the man at the desk, whose previously unflappable demeanor finally flapped and he flinched away. "Where is she?"

"I don't think I should give you that information right now. Maybe you could use a nice refreshing beverage instead."

Honey stepped over the desk and grabbed hold of the man, purple wisps emanating off of her. "You can tell me where she is, or I can tear this station apart piece by piece looking for her."

"Honey," Melissa tried to interrupt but Honey continued unabated.

"I know you have nanites, but I assure you I can tear it apart much faster than they can fix it."

The man's eyes glanced toward his desk.

"Go ahead." Honey eased her grip on the man. "Push whatever alarm you'd like. Silent, loud, it won't make a difference. I'll try not to hurt anyone as I rip apart walls and probably some vital life support systems, but I can't make any guarantees. So you can tell me where she and one person will get hurt, or you cannot, and who knows how many people will get hurt."

"She's in section 227, floor 72, apartment 72304."

"Good boy." Honey patted him on the cheek and turned to Melissa. "I need a ride."

"What is going on?"

"Can you just do what I want this time?"

"I'm not taking you somewhere to kill someone."

"Fine." Honey turned. "I'll walk." Security forces arrived, men and women in blue uniforms with batons, but Honey brushed them aside with a wave of her hand.

Melissa followed Honey, pleading with her, as they made their way through the station. Security forces arrived with increasing levels of weapons, but they did not even slow her down.

A man landed in front of her in a blue and white suit with a blue cape. "I am Supremo Man—," he started to say, but she wrapped him up in purple tendrils and left him on the floor before he could so much as utter a sentence.

The stairs on the other hand, did slow her down as she ran out of breath, sweating and panting on floor twenty-five.

"Ready to talk now?" Melissa asked.

Honey responded with a glare and started to crawl up the steps.

"At least tell me what this is about?"

But Honey said nothing more, even as she collapsed on the seventy-second floor, her dress soaked through with sweat, her limbs unable to move, and her hair a tangle of sweat and frustration.

Another group of security forces tried to seize on the apparent moment of vulnerability, but Honey pinned them to the ground with a wiggle of her pinky.

After a rest period of what Honey guessed to be five minutes but was closer to twenty, she got to her feet and searched apartment numbers until she found the right one. She stared at it, her eyes vacillating between fury and tears. Then she rang the doorbell.

A man answered, middle-aged, dark-skin, balding with a circle of curly gray hair cut short around his head. He wore a colorful sweater and slacks. "Hello there," he said with a big smile. "Can I help you?"

Honey's breath still came heavy as she stared at the jovial man. "Who the fuck are you?"

"I'm Allen, a teacher, I live here."

A voice came from behind the man, one that chilled Honey to her very core. She'd heard the voice countless times, and never thought to hear it again.

"Who is it, Allen?" She appeared beside the man, beautiful and looking about the same age as Honey. Her hair a bright red, her eyes emerald, and a smattering of freckles across her cheeks.

Honey did nothing, a mixture of emotions all hitting her at once. The shock of it all paralyzed her. Then the woman spoke again. "Honeydrops? Is that you? … You look terrible."

Purple energy flared up and Honey charged forward. The charge was wholly unnecessary for someone with magic, but fury took over any practicality. Purple lashes met a purple defensive wall and shattered it. The woman fell backward and Allen ended up flung out of the way. The second attack nearly landed home, but a new shield erected between them and absorbed the blow, this time the color of a soft violet.

Another woman appeared behind Honey's mother, her hand alight with a soft violet glow. She had curly dark red hair, luminous brown eyes, and skin to match. Just as beautiful as the other women in her family. "Who the hell are you?" Honey's half-sister asked.

Honey laughed, mad and wild, even for her. "I see you found yourself a nice little replacement."

"Don't hurt her," Honey's mother pleaded, placing herself between her two daughters. "She's done nothing to you."

This turned out to be the wrong course of action. Seeing her mother show a protective instinct that had never been extended to Honey only made things worse. Honey shrieked, hoarse and devoid of humanity. Power came out in uncontrolled surges lashing at her mother. The two witches tried to stop it, but Honey's power outmatched them. Once, centuries ago Honey had defeated her mother in battle. Since then she'd grown to unrivaled power, and her mother, though powerful in her own right, never even came close to her daughter's abilities. Her sister showed great talent, but not like Honey's. On top of that, the poor girl actually was the age she looked, and thus didn't have centuries of practice. Nor, for that matter, had the girl been so ruthlessly trained in the art.

So, inches from actually dying (instead of faking it), Honey's mother threw herself over her youngest daughter in the vain hopes of protecting her. Fortunately for both, a third entity interceded on their behalf.

The angel received the brunt of the final blow, strong enough that it opened her skin and left a wound where golden magma showed beneath. "Honey, stop!" Melissa said.

Honey did stop, and looked at the wound she'd unintentionally given her lover. Then their eyes met. "Get out of my way, Melicintarifer."

"No, Honey, this is not who you are, not anymore."

"You don't know me. We've spent more years apart than together and you haven't the faintest idea of half the things I've done. I'm just fooling myself thinking I can be anything else."

"No." Melissa stepped forward and put her hands on Honey's shoulders. "You've come so far. I'm so proud of you and all you've done. Don't let her ruin it for you. Hasn't she caused you enough pain?"

"So what? She just gets to live happily ever after now." Tears appeared in Honey's eyes as she choked out her words. "After all that she put me through she gets to be the one who's past it all."

"It's not about her; it's about you. About who you are and who you've chosen to become. I've always loved you, Honey, but now I love being with you. Even if you are the hottest, messiest hot mess who ever was. So please, for my sake if not for your own, stop. Stop hating yourself; stop hurting yourself."

"I don't know how."

Melissa took her lover's face in her hands. "It's OK, we'll figure it out together."

Honey flung her arms around the angel and pulled her into a hug. "I don't deserve you."

"Maybe not, but you're not getting rid of me this time."

"So this is your girlfriend," Honey's mother said.

Honey pulled away and shot venom out of her eyes toward the woman, figuratively speaking. I know that usually goes without saying in novels, but with Honey I needed to clarify. "Yes, she is."

"Not an ideal way to continue the family line, as I taught you."

"Really? That's the first thing you say to me after I just decided not to kill you?"

Alan, having picked himself up off the floor, spoke. "Lovely to meet you both," he said, moving to defuse the situation. "I'm Alan, and this is my lovely wife, Mead, and of course our daughter, Clover."

"Cloe," Cloe said. "It's what everyone calls me." Her eyes were locked on Honey in a mixture of curiosity, awe, and terror.

"Mead has told us all so much about you," Alan said. "Always wondered if we'd ever have the chance to meet you."

"Did she say it might go like this?" Honey asked.

"Yes, she did. Not the part with the angel. That was a bit of a surprise."

"I'm Melicintarifer, but most mortals call me Melissa," Melissa said.

"Wonderful." Alan clapped his hands together. "Will you two be staying for dinner?"

Honey and Melissa shared a glance before Honey asked, "What are you having?"

171

CHAPTER 22

The group of five sat around the dining room table. Well, most of them sat.

"You can sit," Alan said to Melissa.

"My wings make it difficult for me to sit in most chairs. Even if I could, I don't know if I could stop my wings from touching the ground and setting your apartment on fire."

"OK, well, I hope you'll enjoy my tofu stir-fry." He handed her a plate and she took it, standing next to Honey. "So," he said, dishing out food from his wok. "Honey, what have you been up to all these ..."

"Centuries?" Honey offered.

"Yes, centuries. How long has it been exactly since you last saw your mother?"

"Traveling across the cosmos can make you lose track of time. It runs differently in some places, but I'd guess somewhere between six hundred and eight hundred years."

"That's an awfully long time."

"Not long enough," Honey said, picking up a vegetable with her fork.

"Do you hate me so much?" Mead asked.

"Yes." Honey crunched down on the vegetable. "I don't know if words can really express my hatred for you."

Cloe spoke up. "Mom always says you're the most gifted witch who ever lived."

Honey stared incredulous. "She said that?"

"All the time, says you can do things with witchcraft that no human should be able to even dream of."

"That's true, but I find it hard to believe she'd ever say that. Not once in my entire life did she ever say one nice thing to me."

"That's not true," Mead said. "I remember telling you how cute your feet were."

"What? When?"

"After I got done changing your diaper one time."

"When I was a baby?" Honey pounded her hands on the table.

"You said I never complimented you, and I just pointed out that's not true."

"Excuse me then." Honey elongated her words and drenched them in sarcasm. "I guess that makes everything better then."

"She was always like this," Mead said to Melissa. "Overdramatic."

Honey stabbed her fork into the table and Melissa put a hand on her arm. "I'm sorry, Alan, your tofu stir-fry is magnificent, but it's not worth this." She stood up and Mead followed the gesture.

"Come now, Honey," Mead said. "I helped you become the witch you are."

"No!" Honey leaned forward on the table. "I am the reason I became the witch I am. I'm the one who journeyed into heaven and hell and the spaces mortals weren't meant to tread. I uncovered the secrets of the cosmos and bent them to my will. You only ever made me feel like none of that was good enough."

"Which pushed you further."

"You know I used to think you just weren't capable of showing love to anyone, but here you are with a functional family. So why me, Mother? Why am I the one who didn't deserve your love?"

"You think I had a nice childhood. Next to what my mother did to me, you had it easy. We had a duty to carry out our revenge on the world, and I passed that duty onto you. All you ever did was run off on your mad tantrums. I at least tried to do what my mother wanted."

"Oh I did more than that." Honey's hands started to scorch the table as her fury pushed her to the edge of control. "I succeeded, I did everything you wanted and more. I conquered the world and made everyone on it suffer."

"You did?"

"Yes, and it only made my life worse. So I stopped, gave up my evil ways, and restored the world. Now, I spend all my time trying to make up for being the monster you turned me into."

"Good," Mead said. "Good."

"What?"

"I'm glad you gave it up. My mother shouldn't have put it on me and I shouldn't have done it to you. I'm proud of you for moving past it and turning your life around."

No one said anything as glances were exchanged, before Honey spoke up again. "Is that all you have to say?"

"What else is there to say? We don't need to make a scene of it."

"Not make a scene of it?" Honey put a foot up onto the table.

Mead rolled her eyes. "Must you?"

Honey stepped onto the table and pulled her dress down to her waist. "Look at my tits, everybody! I got them out and swinging. Is that too much of a scene for you, Mother?"

"It's a progressive society, Honey; women go topless here all the time. Me and Cloe go for walks in the park, and on hot days we sometimes go topless."

"Walks in the park?" Honey turned and pointed at Melissa. "Take your clothes off, baby, because we are having sex on this table right now."

"Honey." Melissa played with her food. "I'm here for you and I support you, but no."

Honey turned to Alan. "What about you, Alan? I look like my mom; you gotta find this tasty. I'll even call you Daddy if you like."

175

"I better go check on the vegan brownies." Alan left the room for the kitchen.

"Boy or girl?" Mead asked.

"What?" Honey turned on her mother.

"Your boobs are bigger. Good for you; mine went back to their regular size after my pregnancies."

Honey pulled her dress back up and loomed over her mother. "I will not let you within a thousand miles of my daughter."

"What more do you want from me?"

"You could fall to the floor, tearing at your clothes, writhing around and begging for my forgiveness, for a start."

"I'm not going to do that, but I am sorry. I'm sorry for everything. You're right about it all. It's hard not to try and defend myself, but I shouldn't. I could tell you that I've been dealing with my own failings all this time, but you don't need to hear that excuse. I failed you; I'm sorry. I wish I could undo it all and be the mother you deserved but I can't. If you stay, I'll try and do better. It may take some time; change isn't easy, but let me at least try and make up for what I've done."

If there is one thing Honey longed to hear in all those years rampaging across the cosmos, it was this. Yet in hearing it, she felt nothing at all. Honey got down from the table and took Melissa by the hand. "It's too late." They left the apartment together.

"Are you OK?" Melissa asked.

"No, I thought if I heard my mom apologize it would ... I don't know."

"Fix everything?"

"Not that, but I thought it might at least help."

Cloe came out of the apartment after them. "Please don't go."

Honey stopped but did not look at her sister. "It's not that easy."

"I know; she can be a little strict sometimes, but she's getting better. We even go to family counseling."

Honey felt a sudden urge to rip a hole in reality and shove every last thing into it, but she held back. "What did she even tell you about me?"

"She said you were amazing, but that she wasn't the best mother."

"Nothing specific, like how when I almost made a friend at a village fifty miles from our home she tried to force me to sacrifice her in a demonic ritual? Then, when I refused, she wiped out the entire village and made me sleep in the ashes for a week to learn my lesson. Did she tell you she got me a kitten, had me raise it and take care of it then forced me to use that as my first animal sacrifice? Do you know why I first learned how to open a portal to hell? To get away from her."

"She didn't mention all that."

Honey stopped, and regarded her sister. "Are you OK? She's never, say as a nonspecific example, cut off one of your fingers and then let it rot before reattaching it so that it's the worst pain you've ever experienced all so that you can master necromantic magic faster."

"Did she really do that to you?"

"I really don't believe that hurt her more than it hurt me."

"I can't believe she did that to you. She talks so much about how incredible you were. I found myself jealous of you a lot of the time. Not as much now."

"I don't know the woman who's raised you." Honey half reached a hand out to her sister, but couldn't manage it. "But she's not my mother. I'm glad you haven't had to go through what I did, but I just can't. I'm sorry; there's too much for too long. A thousand years could pass with her being the perfect mother and I couldn't forgive her. I'm still picking up the pieces she broke me into. I don't even know if I can fit them back together again."

"I'd still like to get to know you. Maybe I can visit sometime."

"I kinda nearly killed you. Are you sure about that?"

"That's nothing; you should see what our brother did when he found us."

Honey nearly froze in shock once again. "We have a brother?!"

Cloe doubled over with laughter. "I'm just kidding."

"That's not funny, Cloe!"

"Maybe if you'd see your face you'd find it funny."

"Look, I need some time, but I'll think about it."

"OK, you know where we live, so send a raven sometime. Even if you don't want to see me again, I'm at least glad I got to meet you once. I hope you'll send that raven."

"I've got some stuff I need to get back to."

Cloe gave a smirk and started to back away. "Nice to meet you too, Melissa."

"I found the experience unpleasant," Melissa said. "But I hope future meetings will go better."

Cloe turned away and returned home. Honey put her head against Melissa's chest as they walked together. "You want to know the worst part of this whole thing?"

"What?"

"There are people out there who feel the exact same way about me as I do about my mother. I never wanted to become her, but in the worst way possible I did."

Melissa stroked Honey's head. "Some things cannot be fixed and some wounds won't heal."

"Does it hurt?" Honey looked at where her magic had opened Melissa up. The wound had mostly closed already, but a thin line remained visible.

"No, I don't feel pain."

"You don't? Then why are you so into spanking?"

"I like the sound it makes."

"It is a nice sound."

They made their way back to the docks, Honey having to free several groups of trapped security forces. After some apologies, and a brief explanation, followed by a confirmation with Honey's mother, they let her go. It's a good bet that at least part of the reason they were so willing to forgive was that they couldn't stop her anyway.

CHAPTER 23

The *RainbowDeath* arrived back at The Final Stop with an angry, disgruntled witch immediately departing from the vessel.

"Demensios! Get your ass out here! Wait, does he have an ass? Demensios! Get whatever part of you secretes waste out here!"

Melissa followed her off the ship. "I don't think he'll show his face again."

"Motherfucker!" Honey kicked the ground in frustration.

"Come on, we need to find someone who knows something."

They wandered about the station, aimlessly asking people for any information, but no one knew anything. After several hours, an exhausted Honey wandered into yet another bar, and slumped down on a barstool.

"Bartender, I'll have your strongest soda!" She pounded her fist on the bar. The bartender was currently cleaning a glass with a towel slung over his shoulder, as is appropriate for all fictional bartenders. He gave Honey a disinterested look and ignored her.

Honey, at this point, having been stretched to her absolute limit by her confrontation with her mother, did not take the snub well. "Hey, you piece of shit, I'll fucking kill you."

"Honey." Melissa grabbed Honey off of the bar and held her horizontally. "Maybe you're not up for this right now."

"I'm fine; I wasn't actually going to do it."

"I know, Honey, but maybe you need some time to process everything."

"I don't know what good that will do."

A person cleared their throat and the two noticed the entire bar, of what can be described as a rather nasty-looking bunch, gathered around them.

"Oh," said Honey. "It's one of those bars. I could go for a good bar fight."

"Honey, no." Melissa put Honey back on her feet. "We're very sorry to be bothering you all, but do any of you know anything about the Cosmos Guardians?"

A man stepped out of the crowd; a metal plate covered one side of his head with different interface ports on it. One of his eyes was a telescopic piece with a glowing green dot at the center. Both of his legs and one of his arms were robotic. He scratched at the metal plate on his head with his metal arm. "Why do you want to know?"

Honey made a big show of stepping forward. "They kidnapped my daughter so I'm going to kill every last one of them. I'm not supposed to be doing the whole mass murder thing right now, but these are extenuating circumstances."

"No offense, but you don't look like much of a killer. The angel maybe."

"Offense taken. See, things haven't been going great for me since, oh, ever. When I say 'ever' you're probably thinking, she's so young and pretty and I'd love to date her, but I'm actually much older than I look. You might think that after being around for centuries, just fucking once things would be easy, but no, it's always hard. Normally, I'd just have sex until I forgot all my problems, but apparently that's not emotionally healthy so my girlfriend says I can only do it once a day for now. The one good thing I had was my daughter, and those bastards kidnapped her. So either you know something, or you're wasting my time, and you better not be wasting my time." The bar creaked with Honey's last word and a pulse of magic echoed out of her blasting everyone to the floor.

"I have one condition," the man said. "And I'll show you where the Cosmos Guardians are hiding."

"What's that?"

The man got to his feet dusting himself off. "A lot of us here would like to give those sons of bitches what's coming to them. Plus we all liked Alma; don't know how she didn't make it out."

Honey paused, slightly confused how the stranger knew his daughter's name. "Alright."

The *RainbowDeath* departed from The Final Stop with dozens of ships following behind. The ramshackle collection of vessels did not quite look as if they should be holding together. One even had duct tape holding an engine on.

"About these new passengers you've brought on board," Max started.

"What the fuck about them, Max?" Honey responded.

"Never mind."

"That's right never mind." Honey stared far too intently at Max.

"Honey," Melissa said, "can I talk to you in private?"

"If it's about my behavior, no."

"It's not about your behavior."

"Alright then."

Alone in their room, Melissa paced back and forth as Honey sat on the bed.

"You're really only stressing me out more right now," Honey said.

"I've been waiting for the right time to tell you this, and things keep getting in the way. Maybe there just isn't a right time, and now the timing is terrible, but it just keeps getting worse, so waiting isn't helping things."

"Whatever it is, I'll be OK," Honey said.

"You're not OK, right now, and I'm worried about how you'll take this."

"You want to break up, don't you?"

"No, how many times do I have to—fuck's sake, Honey, I'm pregnant."

The word hung in the air, taking time to fully register with Honey. She broke into a big smile and hugged Melissa. "This is so exciting, I have so many questions. Who's the father?"

"You are."

"OK, new line of questioning … How?"

"I don't know, I've never fully understood my own power. Claire forged me to be stronger than even she and there were things she couldn't guide me about. Sometimes my deepest desires, things that I'm not fully aware of myself, manifest. I didn't even have a vagina before I met you."

"What? You never told me that," Honey gasped with uncontained excitement. "Can you grow a penis too?"

"I don't want a penis."

"Come on, I'd grow a penis for you if I could."

"I want that even less."

"Alright, fine."

Melissa caressed Honey's arm. "So … you're happy about this?"

"Of course, we're going to have our own little baby Nephilim."

"I didn't want to add to your stress."

"This is the best news I've had since … since I was pregnant. I had to do that alone while trying to fix the world I broke. We get to do this together. I'm so happy about this. Wait, I just had a great idea. I'd love to carry your child; maybe I could find a way using my magic. I bet I could make it to a D cup."

"Let's maybe just have one pregnancy at a time, OK?"

"Come on, I could be your big titty Goth girlfriend. You could live the dream."

"We can talk about that another time," Melissa said. "It's good to see you happy about something."

"It's good to be happy about something. So is angel pregnancy like human pregnancy? What should we expect here?"

"I have no idea."

"Are you gonna produce milk?" Honey let out an excited gasp. "What does angel milk taste like?"

"Is there a fetish you don't have?"

"No, of course not, why limit oneself? Come, take that armor off, and lie down with me. I just want to hold you for a while."

Alteem would be sitting drinking tea in the cantina as usual, when Honey came in, her eyes intense, and sat down next to him.

"Doing OK?" Alteem said.

"No," Honey said. "I'm not OK."

"I know."

"But I'm really not OK. I just got the best news of my life, and finally caught my breath and I'm realizing just how not OK I am. I'm really not OK, Alteem."

"I know."

"What am I going to do? I need to rescue my daughter, but I'm in no shape to be fighting right now. If I make a mistake, or something goes wrong … I'm past fraying at the edges. The edges are frayed, my core is frayed, I am unwound."

"It'll be OK."

"How can it possibly be OK?"

Alteem put his tea down and put an arm around Honey. "Because you're not alone anymore. We're on a ship full of heroes, plus you've picked up some reinforcements."

"Heroes who hate me. You really think they'll help me?"

"They're heroes, helping people is what they do. Plus I figured it would come to this so I've been working on a great speech. You just relax, take some time with your girlfriend. Here." Alteem pulled out a blanket from behind him. "I traded some of the others for this weighted blanket. You'll love it. Don't worry, I'll take care of everything."

Honey took the blanket and looked Alteem in the eye. "I think for the first time I understand why people followed you."

He patted her shoulder and stood up. "I'm never having sex with you, Honey?"

"Not right now, obviously, I've already used up my one for the day. But come on, you've got to be curious. I'll let you choke me like Mathew."

He ignored her as he walked toward the bridge. Upon arriving he tapped Max on the shoulder. "Mind if I use the intercom?"

"All yours." Max handed him the radio attached to the console on a cord.

"Alright, everyone—"

"You have to push the button there," Max said, pointing to the button.

"Oh, like this?" Alteem pushed the button.

"Yes."

"So they can hear me now?"

"Yes, everything you're saying."

"Great, alright, everyone. It's pretty obvious we're heading into a trap. These people kidnapped Honey's daughter to lure her to whatever they have planned, and you've probably noticed she's not in great shape. She's spent almost two decades running herself ragged trying to make up for past wrongs, and that's a road she'll keep walking. Recent events have not improved things; she's stressed, strung out, and not up for whatever they're planning.

"It comes to us, all of us, to mount this rescue mission. I don't know what they've planned, but it's for the most powerful person in the cosmos. That means this won't be easy, but we're heroes aren't we? When have things ever come easy for us?

"None of you have any reason to want to help Honey. You're all here because she is directly or indirectly responsible for something horrible in your universe. I don't expect you to help her; I expect you to help her daughter. I've gotten to know most of you over the last few weeks, and I hope you think of me as a trustworthy and honorable man. Believe me when I tell you Alma is as good a person as you will ever know. She is worthy of your efforts.

"You came here to be heroes, but couldn't find the person you sought justice against. They called me a hero once, but I don't think I ever deserved that title. Glory is easily earned by fighting villains. In my time, I've learned better that true heroes are those who fight for a world without villains and with no need of heroes.

"The Cosmos Guardians are every bit the villains Honey once was. Some of you have stories of the times they came to your universe. The crimes they committed in the name of their false justice. They kidnap who they want, and if anyone gets in their way, they show no mercy. They appointed themselves the judges of the cosmos, and they've gone unchecked all this time.

"Now we have a chance to stop them. To make sure no more sons and daughters are taken from their homes, and no families are tortured and murdered to take them. We have a chance to be the sort of people we're supposed to be. What will you tell them when you go home? That your journey amounted to nothing? Will you tell them that when the call to fight for justice arrived you refused?

"Most people wish they could have a time to be a hero. A dream born when we're young that we might have the chance to do something good and great in the world. Here is our chance. The time to fight is now; the time for heroes is today. Let us be the people we once dreamed of being. Let us fight to end this bastion of darkness. Let's punch some fascist sons of bitches in their faces.

"We arrive tomorrow. If you want to fight, meet in the hangar; if not, I won't think any less of you."

"Not bad," Max said. "I thought you'd just been drinking tea this whole time."

"Everyone comes to the canteen."

CHAPTER 24

I'd like you to imagine for a moment, if you will, that you'd spent several decades preparing a trap for a bear. Not just any bear, mind you, a monstrous and terrible bear. An unstoppable beast of supernatural strength.

Then, at the time you're expecting this bear to attack, when all your traps are ready to spring and all your plans ready to come to fruition, you are instead attacked by a swarm of wasps.

This is essentially how the Cosmos Guardians felt on the day the *RainbowDeath* arrived at their headquarters accompanied by a fleet of criminal ships that they themselves had once impounded. To compound this disaster, their troops refused to respond to their commands. A thing they'd previously considered impossible when they'd made their perfect soldiers. On top of that, no amount of yelling appeared to make the problem any better, and yelling is the only real skill they'd cultivated in their time.

They did still have their drone fleet, and a great number of automated defenses, but it wouldn't be enough. The officers of the Cosmos Guardians had no choice but to do the things they loved to send others to do. They needed to fight on the front line. A heroic and noble sacrifice that they'd never expected to have to make themselves.

Earlier, I described the attack as a swarm of wasps, but that's not really accurate. Wasps are all the same, whereas this group of people varied from those wielding stone weapons and wearing loincloths, to those with laser guns and plasma throwers. Fireballs were launched from wands and staves, and color-coded groups of five engaged in martial arts. A hundred magical weapons blazed to life with all manner of effects.

Most terrible of them all was the creature that led the assault, the battle angel, Melicintarifer. She flew ahead of the *RainbowDeath* and tore open the hangar doors with her bare hands. The metal turning bright from contact with her skin. The divine radiance that radiated from her rent holes in reality from which poured forth golden flame. Her molten blade cut through any resistance in her path. Her wings sliced apart anything her blade missed.

Watching from his screen, which fizzled out one by one as they melted from the unleashed power of the angel, General Nitrel spoke the words. "Do it."

"But, sir," a nearby officer said. "She's not here."

"It's the only thing that can stop them."

"Yes, sir."

Approximately One Day Earlier

Playing games with the Cosmos Soldiers often proved difficult. The officers could turn their ability to see and hear things on and off at their whim. Even with her own pad, these things could interrupt the games. Once she got the soldiers started they eagerly engaged in the matter, despite the interruptions. It didn't take long for them to become more preoccupied with their games than their duties, eventually giving up their duties altogether.

Alma found herself venturing deeper and deeper into the headquarters as the games spread and antes were upped. The soldiers knew the place well, but she found herself needing to go to greater and greater extremes to find hiding places.

On this day, as she crawled through the vent and popped out the other side, she found a guarded chamber. Of course, since the guards were off playing games it turned into a not-so-guarded chamber. The doors required several layers of codes and eye scans, but opening any door was basic-level witchcraft. It didn't matter how many layers of security they had; bolts could be undone, gears turned, electronics glitched. Alma walked through this incredibly important, should-be, but wasn't, heavily guarded door.

Inside Alma found a tapestry of blood. It covered the walls, the floor, and the ceiling. Witchcraft, Alma knew, of the darkest kind. Runes woven into runes, woven into runes. A cascading spell that needed hundreds of hours of preparation, and the lives of dozens of innocents. A spell wrought out of suffering and torture meant for one purpose: to kill.

The problem with a spell like this, beyond the prep time, is its immobility. To top that off, any disturbance could weaken or even break the spell. Since the spell required such a massive area, keeping it hidden could be near impossible. If one did manage to pull all this off, the spell could indeed kill anyone or anything.

If say, a young witch came across it, said to herself, "I'm going to need a mop," and proceeded to clean up as much of the spell as possible over the course of a day, then it wouldn't do much good at all.

Back to the Present

"Sir?" said the officer.

"Nothing's happened," said Nitrel.

"It's not working, sir."

The officers in the battle conducted themselves relatively well, considering what they were up against. I don't know about you, but I don't think I'd fare very well against a seven-and-a-half-foot angel with giant flaming wings. They were, as previously mentioned, cowards, but being discovered as cowards was their biggest fear. So they fought, and casualties were suffered on either side. They fought in the hangar, their guns firing on the army of heroes and criminals. They fell back to the hallways and fought there. Forcing their foes to take every inch in fighting.

They fought until they realized they could not win, and they realized when alarms began to blare all around the station. A very specific, very terrifying alarm. At first the fighting stopped as the officers looked at each other, not quite believing they'd ever hear this alarm. As soon as the reality set in on them, mass panic swept over the Cosmos Guardians. They surrendered or fled, begging to depart the area as quickly as possible.

Their apocalypse protocol had been activated. The Cosmos Guardians gathered many different prisoners in their time. Some were very guilty, others less so. Once upon a time, the organization served a very different purpose. They considered one type of creature above all to be of the greatest threat to the cosmos, and dedicated themselves to tracking down and eliminating these creatures. When they could not be eliminated they were imprisoned in a shield just out of reality. The apocalypse protocol didn't always exist, but fascists being the parasites they are, slowly took over the organization. Once in charge, they decided that if the Cosmos Guardians' end became imminent, then they'd need to lower the shield in order to ensure the destruction of anyone capable of such a deed.

So they emerged from their prison just outside reality, the thirteen eldritch abominations. The ones too powerful to be killed. Their first goal: revenge on the organization that imprisoned them. They moved toward the headquarters of the Cosmos Guardians. What propelled them through space, who could say, their forms impossible, their existence a defiance of all that is.

On board the headquarters a massive evacuation took place. Those who'd fought moments before ran back through the halls, past the dead, toward ships and escape pods. Some were left behind as those less scrupulous of the criminals did not wait for their ships to fill before departing.

Honey emerged from the *RainbowDeath*, people pushing past her. She heard the sirens and worried something had gone wrong, which it most certainly had. Alma appeared in the hangar, flanked by the Cosmos Soldiers; she spotted her mother, and they ran toward each other.

Honey broke into tears as they hugged. "I knew you'd be OK," she whispered to her daughter.

Melissa appeared beside them. "I don't think we have time for the *RainbowDeath* to get clear. There are too many people who still need to board."

"It's OK." Honey released her daughter. "Everyone fought for me; this time I'll fight for everyone."

Melissa shook her head. "I saw them coming. There are thirteen of them, Honey; even for you that's—"

"I always said if I died I wanted to go killing some eldritch abominations."

"You said you wanted to die having an orgasm so intense that it'd literally kill you."

"Killing eldritch abominations was definitely somewhere in my top five." Honey took her daughter's hand. "Alma, this is Melissa; she's my girlfriend. You two look after each other if I don't make it back."

"Melissa?" Alma said. "I thought you said she's your archnemesis."

"I never said that."

"You said, and I quote—"

"OK, fine, I said it. We parted on bad terms. The truth is we've had an on-and-off relationship and it's been hard, but now we're on again."

Melissa placed a hand on Honey's shoulder. "I'm fighting with you; I should manage at least one or two. I didn't chase after you all this time only for you to die when we were finally starting to make things work."

"No, you have our child inside of you and I don't know if I could keep you safe. I need you to survive this. It'll be easier for me to fight if I'm not worrying about you."

"Honey, I can't lose you."

A portal opened next to them, and from out of it stepped Mead, Cloe, and the man in a blue and white suit with a cape that Honey had swept aside aboard the Guardians of the Cosmos headquarters.

"Mother," Honey said, a bit of purple energy cackling around her. "I believe I said something about killing you if you came within a thousand miles of my daughter."

"Honey?" Mead said. "I guess I shouldn't be surprised. We came because we got the biggest detection of eldritch abominations we've ever seen. We're part of the Guardians of the Cosmos. We guard the cosmos. I'm not here for you."

"You were never here for me."

"Honey, I'm sorry, but there are several eldritch abominations nearby and—"

"Thirteen."

"What?"

"There are thirteen eldritch abominations that should be here in a couple of minutes."

"That's too many, we need to get out of here."

"You need to get out of here, I need to get ready."

Mead stared at her daughter. "You can't, you'll die."

"At least I won't have to deal with you anymore."

"Stubborn, stupid girl. If you're not leaving, then I'm not letting you fight alone."

"I do not want your help."

"You would rather die than let me help you?"

Honey said nothing.

"You can't be serious?" Mead put a hand on her hip.

"I'm thinking."

Melissa pulled Honey to her. "If we all fight, we might win. Please, for my sake."

"I don't want anything from her, even this."

"If you let us fight together, I'll wear the costume."

"You don't mean *that* costume."

"Yes that one."

"OK fine. Alma, get aboard the ship."

Alma gave her mother a nod and left to help people board the ship.

"So we're fighting a bunch of eldritch abominations as a family," said Cloe.

"Just like Louisa and Parnell," Mead said.

"Those books really got off course after volume two hundred," Honey said.

"Spoilers!" Cloe, being young, hadn't had time to read all the books yet.

CHAPTER 25

The smell of rotten eggs filled the air as it tinged a pale shade of green. Pallid flesh bubbled out of the vents and crevices of walls and floors. The flesh rolled toward them through every door and the hangar bay became enclosed with it.

The first of the eldritch abominations arrived.

"What horror?" the man in a cape said.

"What do we do?" Mead asked.

"Fire," said Honey. "Flesh is flesh and it can still burn."

"There's no way we can produce enough fire to destroy this thing," the man in the cape said. "It's practically the size of the station."

"Who the fuck are you?"

"I'm Supremo Man. Super strength, invulnerable, I can fly."

"So you're useless."

"Honey, focus," Mead said.

"Mom, Cloe, take my hands. Melissa, baby, remember that time on Ghelberast?"

"This is hardly the time."

"No, after that."

"Oh right."

Melissa cut a hole in reality in the air above her head. From it poured forth her holy flame. Honey grabbed the hole and put it in front of herself as her sister and mother formed a circle around it. The flesh crept closer around them. The furthest ships that hadn't made it off the hangar started to be enveloped in it.

"Fire of heaven," Honey chanted. "Fire of hell." The golden flame became mixed with red. "I command thee with my spell." A purple tinge appeared on the tips of the flames. "Grow, whirl, burn, and spin. Drown it all in holy sin."

She repeated her chant two more times, with her mother and sister joining her.

The fire turned into a tornado, as the hole in reality spun about and began to move. It bent and twisted as it traveled. The flames grew bigger and bigger as it spun. It burned the flesh to ash as soon as it made contact. The flesh began to retreat as the growing flame chased it down.

As soon as gaps formed in the flesh creatures began to pour forth, each identical to the others. Their skin was red with patches of white, and pointed ears were on the sides of their heads. Their mouths were black and screaming with minuscule grasping clawed hands lining the inside. Each one was about three feet tall. The first descended on a group of officers who hadn't made it out. The officers tried to fight them off with their guns, but any one of the creatures that fell had two more fully formed emerge from its corpse as soon as it died. They grabbed on to the officers with their mouths and the claws inside began to pull the unfortunates slowly inside. Their jaws distended as those caught screamed in terror and pain.

The flames still chasing the flesh sometimes caught a few of the creatures, but even from the ashes two more of them arose. The witches threw spells at them that killed them in all manner of ways, but nothing stopped them from replicating. Melissa's holy sword and Supremo's fist could devastate them, but the replication continued. Nothing worked.

"Dear God, they're horrible," Supremo Man said.

"There's gonna be thirteen of these things; we don't have time for you to be shocked by all of them."

"Sorry, I'm new to this," Supremo Man said.

"I've an idea, but I need my components pouch."

"Honey," said Mead, "I told you to always keep your pouch on you."

"I don't want to hear it. Supremo, how fast can you fly?"

"Supremo speed?"

"What? That's nothing; I've no idea what that means. Just get me to my room on the ship."

Supremo grabbed Honey and they vanished in a blur, only to return a few seconds later. Honey stumbled as Supremo put her on the floor. She bent over and spewed a small amount of vomit. "That's way too fast. I'm so dizzy."

A shadow began creeping across the ground. The light fading as it spread. Melissa lunged for it, and it retreated, but started to move around her. She flew to head it off, but it turned again. She held it back, but slowly it encroached. "Honey, more are coming."

"OK." Honey stepped away from her vomit and dropped to her knees. Grabbing things from her pouch, she smashed them together. After chanting some words in an arcane language, she then tossed the contents into the mouth of one of the creatures charging at her. It fell to the ground and blisters started to form on its body. The blisters popped with a yellow pus and the creature writhed on the floor before dying. Two more creatures emerged, blisters already on their bodies and they ran toward their fellow creatures infecting them. The disease spread this way, the creatures still replicating but chasing each other now as they each died in agony.

From around the corners came yellow tentacles, each larger than the *RainbowDeath*. They wrapped around the entire station and began to squeeze, the inside beginning to scrunch and twist.

"Why does there always have to be something with tentacles?" Mead said.

"I like tentacles," Honey said.

"I know, I walked in on you several times."

"Maybe you should've learned to knock!"

"As if that would stop you."

"We'll never know now will we?"

Cloe shoved past both of them as she began blasting at the tentacles. "Can you two just stop until we're not about to die?"

As the ceiling rent above them a liquid started to drip down, lights dancing inside of it. Any mortal in the area who saw the dancing light walked toward it until they became submerged in the liquid and phased out of existence.

"They're coming too fast," Melissa said, still trying and slowly failing to stop the shadow.

"Damn it," Honey said. "I'm going to do some fae magic."

"Honey," Mead said. "Is that a good idea?"

"You know as well as I do, Mother, it's never a good idea to use fae magic. This is going to hurt everyone, brace yourselves." Honey held out her hands; dancing pink lights appeared in one with dancing purple in the other. She smashed them together and a white flash blinded everyone. Doors did not stop it, walls did not stop it; for half a second everyone went completely blind with white light that burned them down to the core of their being.

The shadow disappeared, and the dancing lights in the liquid were gone, though it still oozed down, now almost invisibly clear. "How's my hair?" Honey asked as soon as everyone blinked the blindness out of their vision.

"The same," Cloe said.

"Thank goodness." Honey breathed a sigh of relief.

The station groaned as the tentacles squeezed it further. "I'll take care of those things," Supremo Man said, flying up into the air and blasting the tentacles with his eye lasers.

"Eye lasers?" Honey said. "How come that wasn't the first thing he said when listing out his powers?"

Supremo tangled with the tentacles as he beat them back.

"He's strong, but not the brightest," Mead said.

"He sure does fill out that spandex though," Cloe said.

"Cloe, he's in his thirties."

"Oh, so I'm not allowed to look?"

"The fates couldn't have sent me one even moderately chaste daughter."

Honey laughed. "You're one to talk, Mom. Where do you think we got it from?"

"I knew it!" Cloe said.

Blood seeped out of the floor. Growing in volume as it churned up from the ground. Whispers came out of the blood, as hands started to reach up out of it. The more of it came, the louder the whispers became and the longer the reaching hands.

Honey nudged Melissa. "It's just like me at a certain time of the month."

Melissa gave Honey a flat look.

"Come on, not even a giggle?"

Melissa scooped Honey up and lifted her out of the blood. Honey watched as the blood enveloped Cloe and Mead who stood back to back, bloody hands grabbing at them.

"Damn it." Honey gave Melissa a quick kiss before leaping out of her arms into the blood. Inside the whispers felt like they were coming from the inside of her head. In a sea of red she saw people reaching out for her, begging for help. People she knew, voices she knew, her daughter, her friends, her lover. They screamed and choked on blood as they pleaded for her.

Honey thought of flames to burn the blood, but the blood rose too quickly. A void to drain it would be too easy to escape. It finally occurred to her that blood is a good source of power for witchcraft. Why should sentient blood be any different?

She started a summoning spell, using the blood as fuel. It resisted her, pulling against her, but she pulled back harder. It came to her, like a sheet of red being dragged inward. Scratching runes on the ground they started to soak up more of the blood, the hands reaching from the blood tried to grab on to things to keep from being absorbed, but it did them no good. The blood receded into the spell, and into the runes.

"Mew," the white fluffy kitten said sitting in the place the blood runes had once been. The faintest sound of an abominable whisper echoed from its mewling.

"Kitty," Cloe said, running over to grab it up.

"Need a familiar?" Honey asked.

"I'm going to name him Professor Paws."

"Just to be clear, that's not really a kitty; it's a familiar with the power of an eldritch abomination. You have to take good care of it. Not even my familiar is that strong."

Cloe nuzzled the kitty against her face.

The *RainbowDeath*'s engines fired to life and began to turn in the hangar.

From outside appeared a mass of red flesh, grabbing and slithering along the walls. Where it moved it left behind a trail of red flesh that grew and crept along the walls. From both the creature and the trail sprouted reaching, licking tongues. Each tongue had several smaller tongues on it, which each had their own tongues. Where they touched they spread rust and rot.

"Well, hello," Honey said with a flirty toss of her hair. The creature opened up around a circle of flesh ridges and spewed forth a bile of red and yellow on Honey. It ate the ground around her, but her magic protected her. "I can work with that."

"Honey, no!" Melissa said.

"Fine." Honey started to swirl her hand creating a purple glow. Spreading outward around her the floor mended itself.

From the other side of the station came a crunching noise as a collection of gnawing fish heads emerged. The fish heads protruded out of the mouth of a gigantic angler fish. As the creature came further into view the angler fish hung out of the mouth of an even bigger frog, which in turn hung out of the mouth of a human head cut off at the neck with gore trailing out of it. Each of its maws drooled and the stench of rotten fish filled the room.

Melissa took wing and charged the creature. Around her fissures in reality opened and poured flame at the creature. It lurched forward, the fish shooting out, each half-eaten, attached to the angler by stretching intestines. They tried to swallow her as they shot out, swimming on the air before retracting. She tried to slice them, but even her blade did not pierce their flesh. She dodged around them, her flame pouring into their mouths leaving them unburned.

She grabbed on to one of the heads as it retracted, and as she got close to the angler portion of the body its lure lit up. Any mortal would be finished in that moment, but Melissa was no mortal. She sliced it, but it too proved too thick. The frog's tongue oozed out from between its lips and the angler. It lashed for her, but she dodged around it and flew behind the monster.

She lunged for the open rear of the human, but from out of it came a swarm of creatures with the bodies of frogs and the heads of piranhas. They surged for her, leaping out like a plague, but she flew out of their grasp and sent forth her holy flame to cleanse them. They did not prove as immune to it as fish were. Still they swarmed out in an endless tide, and she surged forward in fire, burning her way into the neck of the human head. She disappeared inside. The dead eyes of the human lit up, then the whole thing erupted into a golden inferno.

Meanwhile, Honey worked on her spell as its counter effects pushed the tongue monster back. Another creature emerged from one of the holes rent into the space station. A collection of eyes surrounded one gigantic eye at the center. Claws stretched along each eye, digging into it as they stretched, squeezing them until they bled and bulged. Inevitably they would pierce the eye causing it to pop spewing a bloody pus around them that fizzed the ground away. A new eyeball would spring out, the dead one discarded as it did so.

Mead and Cloe joined one hand each, holding the free one toward the creature. Violet chains erupted from the ground, pinning the creature down. As it strained against the chains its eyes sprang free and ran across the ground on nerve endings. They traveled as far as they could before the claws would pop them.

The two witches held the creature as Honey finished her spell. A spreading restoration spell that undid the damage to the station. The tongue creature tried to flee but the spell hit it, unmaking it and leaving behind a pile of loose tongues.

"Such a waste." Honey wiped a tear from her eyes.

"Honey," Mead said as she and Cloe strained against the eye monster.

Honey held out a hand and a blast of purple energy three times her height evaporated the eye creature. A swarm of skittering spiders emerged from several cracks in the station. They swarmed together in a writhing mass of spiders that took the shape of a giant spider. A few stragglers were swarmed by spiders and left webbed and filled with poison. Honey vaporized it with another purple blast. "I thought this would be harder," she said.

Melissa returned to their side. "It's not over yet."

Supremo returned from outside, covered in viscera. "The tentacle creature is dead."

The station shuddered. Tearing through the recently restored wall came metal jaws. Its eyes glowed red, its mouth a furnace, its head the shape of a lizard. A machine claw wrenched away one of the walls.

"What the?" Honey said.

"Oh," Supremo said. "You can be surprised by them, but I can't."

"It's a robot; eldritch abominations aren't robots."

From the other side of the station another two metal hands tore open the wall. Its head poked through, a metal skull with lenses for eyes. The humanoid robot came into the hangar.

"Someone made these," Mead said.

"Who would make eldritch abominations?" Honey held up a hand that started to glow purple.

The two robots charged each other. Metal hands wrestling with metal hands as mechanical roars sounded.

"People who wanted to destroy each other," Mead answered.

Honey lowered her hand. "I say we let them fight."

Their fists met in the air, and reality shook. Things blinked out of existence around the hangar.

"Who knows what damage their fight might do to the cosmos," Melissa said. "We have to stop them."

"I swear, every time I get close to watching two giant robots fight, something ruins it." Honey fired another blast at the lizard robot. It staggered back, but showed no sign of damage. "Tough sons of bitches."

The human robot grabbed the staggered lizard and slammed it to the ground. The hangar split into two realities for a moment, before coming back together. "We need to keep them apart," Supremo said.

"And find a way to destroy them," Mead added.

Supremo flew up and grabbed the human robot, dragging it away as it struggled against him. Honey held out a hand, and Melissa grabbed it, taking her into the air. The witch sent blast after blast to the lizard, which reeled from the attacks, falling back.

"How do we destroy them?" Melissa asked.

"Easy," Honey said. "If we can get them to stay still."

"I can't hold it," Supremo said, and the human robot escaped his grasp.

Mead and Cloe threw up chains around it, but it tugged against them and both witches went to their knees. "We can't hold it long."

"I've an idea," Honey said. "Supremo, give me a minute. Melissa, the floor."

Supremo went into a losing battle with the lizard bot as Melissa landed on the ground. Honey took her hand, and sliced it open with some magic. Using the angel's blood she wrote runes on the floor.

"Maybe I'm misreading what you're doing," Melissa said. "But it looks like you're about to try sending one of these robots to heaven."

"I don't think so. It went to the heaven of the universe we were in. Hypothetically if we were in a different universe it'd go to that universe's heaven. Right now we're in between universes."

"So where will it go?"

"I have no idea." Honey let out a maniacal laugh.

Mead and Cloe fell to the floor as the human robot broke free of their chains.

"Get ready." Honey held out her hand for Melissa. The angel took it and Honey slammed her hand into the ground. A portal opened up as the human robot charged forward. Melissa lifted the two to safety as the robot fell into blackness. The parts of it that went through the portal vanished, not appearing on the other side. It reached out its hands to try and grab the edge, and succeeded. Before it could do anything else it disappeared into the void and the portals closed. Only its fingers clutching at the edge remained.

The reptile bot tossed Supremo aside one final time. The man struggled to his feet, but collapsed back to his knees. The reptile looked around, and seeing only the fingers it charged at them, smashing its fist into them over and over again.

Melissa put Honey down and the witch reached out her hand toward the robot. A purple mist drifted over to it as it hunched down smashing the fingers. The mist worked its way into the seams of the body, disappearing where it moved but finding a way through its innards.

"And …," Honey said. "Power source." She clutched her hand and the robot stiffened before collapsing. With a wave of her hand the mist dismantled the robot into a pile of metal.

"Where did that portal lead?"

"As far as I could tell, nowhere."

Mead, helped Cloe to her feet and they shuffled toward Honey. "Is it over?" Cloe mumbled. Supremo struggled to his feet, bloody and bruised. Even Melissa had some scrapes where her golden blood shone through underneath.

Honey dusted off her hands, not even out of breath. "How many was that? I wasn't counting."

A black dot appeared in Honey's vision, so small she thought it was a bug at first and tried to wave it away. It darted around her hand and disappeared inside her head.

CHAPTER 26

Floating in darkness
    Alone
    To move hurts
To think hurts
But in the darkness there is peace if one does not resist
But if you do not resist the darkness, you only sink deeper

She struggled to open her eyes, the pressure pushing back against her. It hurt, but they opened. Everything hurt, everything but the darkness.

Even with her eyes open, she saw nothing, and felt only the pain. She knew if she stopped resisting, the pain would go away. Something kept her moving, the idea that the darkness might end, that the pain might end with it. So she walked in the darkness.

It did not matter how long she walked; the darkness refused to abate. The pain on the other hand, grew. Each step became harder to take than the last. The pressure grew, pushing her down. She wanted to stop; she wanted to close her eyes and curl up in the peace of the darkness. To give in to the darkness was the only way to make the pain end.

Still, she persisted, until each step felt like a burden, and each breath troubled her. A voice came out of the darkness. Her own voice, soothing and subtle.

"Why are you still fighting?"

"I have to get out of here," Honey said to herself. "I have to get out of the darkness."

"You know it won't end. It never ends. We struggle on, thinking we can get out, thinking there's still hope for us, but I know better. There's no hope, only the darkness, and it's easier not to resist."

"You're it. The thirteenth one."

"No. I'm us, I'm me, I'm you. It's all the same."

Honey appeared before herself. Staring into her own eyes, but not her own. These eyes were peaceful. They didn't carry her hurt, her sadness, her pain. These eyes surrendered to the darkness. She spoke to herself. "You're a trick. I have to beat it."

"No, all it did was isolate us. Let us be alone, finally."

"I don't want to be alone."

"I know, keep everyone around. Chase the darkness away, but, it doesn't work does it? We keep moving, keep talking, keep slutting around. We do everything, but we can't stop, because then there's just this. It's OK. It's going to be OK. This is what we needed, to stop, to see the truth. Just you and me, just us, just you."

"No."

She stroked her own cheek. "It hurts, so let's stop fighting. It's time to face me."

"I'm not you."

She squinted at herself. "But you are; we know that. We try to believe them when they lie to us. They pretend, because if they don't they fear what we might do. They pretend to love us, to believe in us, to care about us. They don't; I know the truth: They don't care about you, don't love us. How could they love a monster?"

"You're the monster."

She nodded. "Yes. We are."

Gesturing around herself, visions appeared in the darkness.

She saw herself destroying armies, laughing with glee. People running in terror as their village was destroyed with her cackling the whole time. People tortured as she looked on with delight.

Honey took a step back. "I'm not that person anymore."

"That's the lie they tell us, the one we want to believe. They make excuses for us and we so want it to be true. I know better. You know we're still her; we always have been, I always will be."

"No." Honey turned and ran, but the visions followed her. The worst were the ones that didn't matter. She destroyed and killed not because she had to, but because of the convenience. Those she never needed to kill at all. Those she killed only because she could.

"Stop!"

"You're the only one who can stop it."

She stopped, and everything returned to darkness.

"Isn't this better for us? Hasn't it gone on long enough? Don't you prefer the darkness?"

"I keep trying, I keep failing, and trying again."

"And failing again."

"Why do we keep on fighting, fooling ourselves into thinking we can escape? There's is no escape from the dark, but it's better if we just stop."

"Give in."

"No, I won't."

"Yes I will, eventually. How long do you want to keep playing pretend?"

"Everyone is better off without us."

"I can still do some good."

"It doesn't matter; nothing we do matters."

"We only ever made things worse."

"No, I'm not evil anymore."

"I remember the worst of us; let me show you."

"No, please."

She bent over the body, its blood draining into the runes she'd dug into the ground. The dagger in her hand, a thin silver thing, with a cross guard that widened at its end. Elsewhere she saw the mother, sobbing over an empty crib. She saw hundreds of mothers.

Then her daughter's face hovered before her. Honey fell to her knees, the dagger still in her hands. "Stop!" she said again, and held the dagger to her throat.

"Do it," she said.

"I've wanted to do it for a long time."

"Aren't you just, so, tired?"

"Tired of every day being a struggle."

"Tired of every day being so hard."

"End it, finally."

"Then it won't hurt anymore."

She felt and saw the blood draw as it pressed against her neck.

"It's what we deserve."

A blade cut through her wrist, bright and molten. Her hand fell with the dagger still in it and the darkness cleared. In front of her she saw Melissa, her sword in hand.

"You cut off my hand!" she screamed at the angel.

"Honey, can you hear me?"

"You cut off my hand. That hurt."

"You can reattach it."

Honey's hand dropped the dagger and crawled over to her. Hopping back onto her wrist. The darkness began to creep back in. She felt panic grip her. "No, I don't want to go back."

"Honey." Melissa grasped Honey's head and looked her in the eye. "What's happening?"

"Help."

"Look at me." An urgency appeared in Melissa's face that Honey had never seen before. "Whatever happens you never do. Do you understand me? You never—"

Melissa's voice vanished and Honey's face followed as the darkness surrounded her again.

"She can't save you," Honey said, standing before herself again. "We want her to, we want to believe she can. In the end, I know she can't save us. It was nice though, wasn't it, playing pretend for a while? Dreaming someone could actually love us. I'm so stupid sometimes."

"I love her."

"She says she loves us, but she doesn't know us. If she did there's no way she'd say that, if she really knew everything we'd done. No one could love us; no one should."

"No."

"Stop lying to yourself. It's time to be honest."

"This isn't me; you're not me. I'm better now."

"Why do you keep hurting us?"

Another vision appeared, this time of Melissa looking at her the way she so often did, disappointed. "Honey, I'm sorry, but I just can't." Then she left. Again and again the visions appeared, each from a different moment.

"Honey, I can't."

"Honey, I'm sorry."

"Why can't you just stop?"

"Why would you do that?"

"Honey, you went too far."

"No matter how much I try, you never listen."

"This is never going to work, is it?"

"I love you, but maybe that's not enough."

"I'll never be the person you need, and you'll never be a person I want."

"Enough! I'm through with you forever!"

Honey's hand tipped up her own chin. "Like I said, she's better off without us. They all are."

"We've hurt them too many times, all of them, and we're just going to hurt them again."

"It would hurt them if I did it."

"They'd be relieved."

"They wouldn't have to deal with us anymore."

"Sigh at us."

"Frown at us."

"Tell us to stop."

"It's better for everyone."

"You won't have to hurt anyone anymore. We won't hurt anymore."

That dagger could still be seen on the ground. Glittering in the dark. She reached for it.

"No, not with your hand. They can stop you that way."

"I need to do it in a way they can't stop me."

"I have a daughter."

"She left you."

"She doesn't need me anymore."

"No one ever needed you."

"Melissa is pregnant; I need to be there for her."

"They don't want you around, screwing things up. Doing everything wrong."

"Like I always do."

"Isn't it enough already? Hasn't it been enough?"

"You only make things worse, for everyone."

"Making the same stupid mistakes over and over again."

"I never learn."

"You'll never learn."

"I'm just so tired."

"End it; end all the pain."

"The pain I feel, the pain I cause."

She reached out with her power, a purple glow lifting the dagger into the air. It's all she could see in the darkness, the thin silver line aimed straight for her heart.

Some part of her remembered that even if all she saw was the darkness things still existed outside of it. Melissa cut off her hand, but she hadn't seen it, or felt anything before it happened. She must have been holding on to her hand, trying to pry the dagger away from her. Cutting off her hand merely as final desperate attempt to stop her.

"She can't save you," she told herself.

"But I don't want her to save me."

"Don't lie."

"It's not a lie. I want to be the person who can make her happy."

"You'll never be that person."

"You aren't good enough."

"You're an idiot."

"Saying the wrong things all the time."

Melissa must still be trying to stop her.

"Don't let them stop you."

"They don't really care about me."

"It's just to be nice; they pretend."

They're there, wanting to save her. Out beyond the darkness. Mead, Cloe, Melissa, Alma, maybe others by now. She could not see them, she could not feel them, but they were there for her.

"You aren't just me."

"Not this again. Stop lying."

"It's not a lie. You're something else too. I know these thoughts are mine, but it's not just me."

"No one can save you."

Honey looked at herself in the eyes. "Who else will you hurt once I'm gone? Who will you go after next?"

"You'll only hurt them more if you stay."

"Will you go after Melissa? My sister? My daughter? Who else will you hurt?"

"You're the one who hurts them, causes them pain."

"I won't let you, I won't let you make me hurt them."

"You can't escape me, I am you."

"No, I can't, but I can stop you from hurting anyone else."

"It's you! You're the one who hurts everyone."

It hurt to fight the darkness; it hurt to do anything in the darkness. A thousand hands reached out from Honey, grabbing the darkness.

"Stop fighting!"

They dragged it toward Honey, pulling it back to her. More hands appeared, each one hurting more, taking more effort. Grabbing the endless darkness and dragging it to her. Thousands of hands, tens of thousands, gripping the darkness. She bent it to her will, and the pain grew so much she could not move or think. A dull ache pushed back against her the more she pushed back against it.

How long it went on she did not know; it felt like forever. An endless pain that only grew. It didn't hurt like a cut or a bruise. Just a pressing that did everything to stop her. She forgot about the darkness, and her world became that pain, as endless as the darkness before it. Still she fought, knowing that if she failed it'd hurt those she loved, and she'd hurt them too much already.

Her vision cleared, the pain dimmed, but did not vanish. She saw Melissa first, standing between her and the dagger, which still floated in the air. Alma had her arms around her neck and hugged her close. Cloe and Mead erected a magic shield to try and stop the dagger. Others had exited the *RainbowDeath*. Max and Jack were trying to destroy the dagger with their blasters. Alteem set up physical barriers between her and the dagger.

She let it drop, and it vanished when she did so.

"Mom?" Alma said, and she put a hand on her daughter's arms.

Melissa turned around and their eyes met.

"It's over," Honey lied.

"What happened? Are you OK?"

Honey opened her mouth to say something, but only tears came as she shook her head.

EPILOGUE

Nothing lasts forever, but everything else doesn't. As far as we know, nothing might not last forever either.

So it is, five seals were made, and five seals were broken. The last to fall was a prison to many creatures. It changed hands more than once, and its final owners split in two. Those who remained forgetting the original purpose for which it had been built.

The old seals that held it in place were destroyed. They were restored, but they broke long enough for the prisoner to escape. Now he rose from the black pool that held him. A tiny universe made just to imprison him.

Lipstick a blood red. Pale blond hair hung down his back with dark tan skin. Three red straps covered his chest and wrapped around his neck. They extended from the scarlet skirt that clung tightly to his lower body. His eyes opened for the first time in thousands of years, red and bloody.

Some might say there is always a bigger fish, always someone better, but there must be a biggest fish and someone or something is always the most powerful in the cosmos. Once upon a time, it was he.

His empire stretched across universes, spreading through the cosmos. Now the work began again.

ABOUT THE AUTHOR

Dear reader, I have been advised that my previous about the sections were too boring and dry and that I should try and inject some of my humor into them. The problem with this is that I absolutely loathe talking about myself. If no one ever knew anything about me, I would be delighted. Except we're supposed to connect with our readers now, thanks internet.

I'm from North Dakota and there are plenty of quips to made about my home state, but I don't need to add to them. ND doesn't need me ragging on it, plenty of others already do. In my younger years I very much hated this state, but I'm older and wiser. I have, at the very least, come to appreciate it for what it is. It's not for me, it never would be. I don't fit in here, I dare say I wouldn't fit in anywhere, but I especially don't fit in here. People like fishing, camping, and hunting, while I like not doing those things. It's a wonderful place, it has its beauty, its wonders, but we'll never fit together. I did try to like fishing, but when you spend your time fishing hoping not to catch a fish so you can keep at your book, one realizes they don't actually like fishing and instead just likes reading by the lake. I own a rather clean tackle box, quite dusty though.

There will be a Witch'n 3, unless a comet destroys the Earth or something. I suppose that's generally something that goes without saying. I'll pick you up tomorrow, unless the sun explodes. People would understand, you don't have to tell them, yet I often feel the need to. I'm not sure if it's a weirdly specific insecurity or just the pedant in me. Beyond Witch'n 3 I have a couple of ideas for spin offs. One I'd actually like to write before Witch'n 3, but I can't because it wouldn't make any sense until after. I'd also love for Jack and Max Stallion to get their own book, I just don't know what it's about yet.

Finally, I would like to ask, as we must, that you might leave a review for this book. I know, we all hear it again and again. The reason we do, however, is that it is enormously helpful, especially for us little indie authors. So I ask, please.

www.ingramcontent.com/pod-product-compliance
Lightning Source LLC
Chambersburg PA
CBHW022016170626
46808CB00001B/434